TASMAN'S
TRAVAIL

Tasman's Travail
The Journey Down Under

iUniverse books may be ordered through booksellers or by contacting:

iUniverse
1663 Liberty Drive
Bloomington, IN 47403
www.iuniverse.com
1-800-Authors (1-800-288-4677)

ISBN: 978-1-4759-7926-8 (sc)
ISBN: 978-1-4759-7927-5 (ebk)

Library of Congress Control Number: 2013903732

Printed in the United States of America

iUniverse rev. date: 02/26/2013

TASMAN'S TRAVAIL

THE JOURNEY DOWN UNDER

JEFFREY UNDERWOOD
&
KATE TAYLOR

iUniverse, Inc.
Bloomington

CONTENTS

INTRODUCTION

The Dutch East India Company is in the throes of expansion. They are seeking gold, treasure, land to conquer and an easy passage to South America. Still in thrall to the invisible Hand of his Overlord, the long lived vampire entity is compelled to find new skin. And he does exactly that.

This book is another segment in the entity's evolution toward the light. And he finds himself suddenly in the guise of Abel Tasman, Master Commander and brave explorer, who becomes the first European to espy the sites of Van Diemen's Land, eventually Tasmania, and of New Zealand. It is sixteen hundred and forty two and white man's expansion is in full throttle.

Much of this book, as with the others of the Entity Saga, rides true facts and historical details of the early European discovery in the South Seas. In it, uncover the often calamitous influence of white colonialism on the indigenous peoples. Be also exposed to the early myths and cultures of the Maori and the Moriori. And why the Moriori went into near absolute decline. And discover the nature of cannibalism as it was practiced then.

As the entity goes, so goes his undead cohorts from books past. They are all lovely to behold but are captives of their undead fate. And, most surprisingly, not all vampires relish their existence. The ambivalence among them grows and tamer threads weave with the vicious.

New Zealand is revealed as a beautiful country consisting of two large islands, north and south. Mountains, glaciers, volcanoes, lagoons and lush and sweeping plains arise as the story unfolds and the characters are fully revealed.

The entity comes face to face with a demon more powerful than he. Except for his master, this is impossible ... or so he believes. He is dumbfounded at realizing that this she-demon has destroyed some closest to him. And is she capable of eliminating the incomparable entity too?

The romance of the virgin territory, the vital history and the erotic permutations of the characters will put a spell on you. Once that spell has you almost within its grasp ...

Only then, let this tale sink its fangs into your flesh and soul.

ACKNOWLEDGMENTS

The Blend of Jeff and Kate's Interweaving is a Blessing.

Also, Thank You for Your Character Inspiration:
Rose Smith & Ellie Mackay.
Our Families for Loving Us Through the Spice.

To Brave Abel Tasman Who Explored Where Others
Would Not.

To All Cultures, Especially Peaceful, Which Fascinate K & J.
To the Entity Who Is Always Evolving Toward the Light.
To His Master Who Insists Upon That However Subtly.

Finally Our Heartfelt Appreciation to iUniverse.
They Make Our Words, These Books, Possible.

CHAPTER 1

Hell Bent

Janna, once known as Minkitooni, was hell bent on rejoining her love. He was skin again and he had signaled her to come be with him. His merger was with one named Abel Tasman.

The year was sixteen hundred forty two and the summoning call had shot from Batavia, Indonesia seventy two hours ago. This ping of knowledge from him had, at long last, filled the void which had been her bleak soul since he had departed her in the far flung and long decimated Mississippi River region of North America. She was ecstatic and rushed to him without a moment's hesitation. He was hers and she meant to always have him.

He had asked her to hold her impatience though while he oriented himself to surroundings that were starkly new and unfamiliar to him. It would not take long as he had become accustomed to finding balance with each fresh habitation.

In the meantime, she found her name that fit this Dutch culture. Asians had been allowed only outside of the fortified city. So she had not had to worry choosing a mixed name of any kind. Janna had seemed appropriately Dutch and she had taken it for herself confidently.

Once several centuries ago, her lover had given all his compatriots a sliver of a gift. It had turned out to be a gift of immense proportions. He had shared a piece of himself that allowed her to immediately understand the language that engulfed her in each place that she found herself. She had begun as a high born princess and then queen of Gaelic heritage, morphed into a statuesque North American Indian princess connected to a prominent chieftain and was now absorbing the Dutch identity so that she blended harmoniously with the teeming citizens of this city.

Shadows exerted their dominion over this walled city in the hour just trailing the sun's disappearance. Strangely, as if girding for onslaught, the wall that completely surrounded the metropolis of Batavia had a second fixture, a moat, that lay just beyond the wood structure. Prior, when she had flown over both, she had seen, in the last instant of being airborne, the canals of muddy and somewhat dank waters that crisscrossed the cities interior domain and divided that area into smaller and smaller segments. And the Ciliwung River appeared as a blue spike that cut the heart of Batavia in two. It was the sole source that fed the web of existent canals there.

If she were not vampire, she would have trembled in fear at walking alone through the embrace of the city. She was statuesque and tall, as were many of the other female Dutch inhabitants of Batavia, but she was alone and unaccompanied. That was what made her stand out immediately. This was not done unless one was ill bred and negligent. And if one were either, then that female was considered prey by those who sought to wickedly intrude.

But her demon's status rendered her without fear. And that invincibility shone through her eyes and froze any would be aggressors in their place. If not by her look alone, a subtle hiss or a glint of fang was always a proven remedy of last resort. She, after all, did not want to give away her secrets to anyone, stranger or friend.

Her attire had been matched to the Dutch trends of the day. This had been accomplished when she had first arrived. Her lover had spoken to her in his thoughts and told her to go to a particular inn, procure a particular room in that inn and find a satchel of his sitting atop the bed provided. He had filled this satchel with all the necessary garments that she was presently bound up in. And bound she felt after having worn nearly no clothing as the Cahokia chieftain's companion, Minkitooni.

The appearance that she offered up as she strode the storefront boardwalks was flawless and of utter and beautiful perfection. She had thrown a woven shawl over her shoulders as she had to have an item to cover her while she explored the outdoors. It was not cold but it was etiquette's necessity. Beneath the wonderfully delicate shawl was a long slim gown that conformed precisely to all fashion nuances demanded. She wore this gown, a requirement for formal or informal moments, which had a long vertical line that slid down nearly to the wood slats beneath her fashionable shoes. It also had a low curving and sensual horizontal emphasis at the bodice which dropped below both shoulders. The material that fanned out in loose sleeves was longer and tighter than was customary. Yet she was aware that the new trends followed her present apparel.

Her cleavage was having difficulty surrendering to the confines of the clothing's press. Here was where she felt thoroughly captive to her clothing. Her curves were tightly corseted and she had to concentrate in order to fill her lungs sufficiently. It was unfortunate in these circumstances that her bust was of proportions that were utterly voluptuous.

This was a further reason for her to slowly inhale to her fullest capacity. Otherwise, she might faint from a lack of adequate oxygen.

Finally, below the constricted area of bust and waist, the sumptuous gown was drawn back and pinned up to display the intricately and heavily decorated petticoat.

She felt as if she moved beneath the weight of the world.

Whoever had designed these heavily redundant, almost crushing items, if it were a man, he might want to try them himself and feel the torture. If it were a woman who designed them, shame on her sadistic nature that had nary an ounce of mercy within her.

In spite of the clutch of her clothing, she certainly was absorbing the wonders of the South Pacific quickly. This was her third night of exploring the layout here. Batavia had been built to the specifications of an enterprise titled the Dutch East India Company. This was their outpost to investigate the southern world for trade and profit.

But she was ready to return to the inn and find her way to pitch these clothes from her nearly desperate body. She had sacrificed enough for the better good of assimilation for herself and her lover.

The inn took but a moment to arrive at. She ignored the leering patrons as she made haste to her room. The din vanished as she closed her door. She took the affixed metal bolt and drew it snugly into its latch. That would do. And if not, she would come to her own rescue.

She so desired that layer upon layer of her outfit simply fall to the dusty old oak floor. But she knew that she had to gently fold and neatly lay all so that no dirt or wrinkles might show upon the rewearing.

She was most comfortable wearing nothing at all. And that is exactly what she did while she anxiously awaited her lover's silent call that was to beckon her to his precise location.

Unconsciously, she cupped her magnificent breasts and nonchalantly stroked her swelling nipples, feeling the pulse in her Venus vault and ruby jewel throb higher and higher.

CHAPTER 2

Route Out

His passion for her had come to a crescendo and he was unable to handle separation any longer. His blend into the culture, even if not perfect yet, was complete enough for his taste; because his taste for her was to have her instantly. He was hungry, no starving, for her embrace, for the touch of her silken and flawless skin and to dwell in the palace that was her luxuriant high heat.

The rustle of air gave Janna an immediate prickling sensation and she became intensely aware then that she did not have to go to her lover. He was behind her and lifted her long braid which she had woven for her nightly comfort. In a daze, she began to fondle herself again and clenched her thighs automatically upon his touch. When he kissed her at neck nape, grazed his sharp fangs along that sensitive swath of skin and breathed hot and ragged panting breath on her, it was then that wetness exploded between her legs. Her torrent of excitement carried an urgent pulse with it that was not to be denied.

He turned her as she sat and she saw Abel for the first time ever. But it was not Abel that she sought; it was the creature within this man who she was deeply in love with. This love had been ever huge and constant for centuries. She had first burned for him, a yearning that was too compelling to describe, in Scotland eight hundred years ago.

She stroked her thick, rapidly firming and lengthening raspberry stained tips in a more frantic motion. She flicked them under the weight of her thumbs but was helpless and had to also squeeze and twist them harshly. He took them from her and pulled on them hard, over and over. She gasped for him and her dew slicked inner thighs showed as she lifted her hips and clenched and unclenched her thighs rhythmically.

Having hissed through her open window, then having transformed himself into human form, he had his linen doublet still hanging from his massive chest. The buttons were undone to the point of his waist and his hirsute torso expanded and contracted fully in his eagerness. Janna lunged for his open garment and ripped it from his body. She took his nipples in hand and pinched them hard and repetitively. She chose to have him experience what she was experiencing.

He remained standing before her, tormenting her nipples to a level that almost hurt it was so delicious to Janna. But too, she spied his legs slightly flexed, very wide spread and his bulge thrusting upwards toward her. His organ stretched the material enclosed around his libido's core. She was unable to resist and, breath rasping, she reached to slash the cloth into shreds. He clasped her wrist at this moment and peered into her lust glazed eyes.

"We have little time before we sail; early this morning to be exact. So I must leave us both unfulfilled. Our desires will build and it will be so good later."

A small moan and whimper fell out of her mouth. She begged him, "Just a taste of you. Please, oh please."

She loosed one of her hands from his grasp and used the outside flat of her fingers to rub his bulge up and down. She felt the tension within his column and she meant to firm it up more so. She was not about to miss putting her lips to his enlarging cock.

Chagrined, he replied, "You are just too fucking convincing my love! Feel me on your tongue and hand while I attempt to explain to you the circumstances surrounding our new life."

Both he and she reached for the ties which kept him contained and the flurry of their effort sprang his thick erection to her moist and tantalizing lips. His shaft was of a length so that she fisted it as she guided it deeply into her mouth. His mushroom shaped cockhead, plum colored as well, was tightly lodged in her mouth with her tongue licking and swirling and probing for his clear dew. She sucked this clear liquid avidly and swallowed it many times as it continued to flow under her ministrations.

His thighs quivered and he emitted a small growling moan of approval. With shaky breath, he began.

"I work for a very powerful Dutch company now. Their principle station is here in Batavia. Batavia is a launching point and route out for exploration of the more southern oceans. They intend to find land that will give up gold, silver and valued resources to make my superiors rich. They also wish to discover if there is a passage of some kind to lead them to rumored territory across the seas here.

"Oh my love, I am so close to release and the damnable close of my explanation too. Which will come first? Ahhhhhhhh!" He panted hopelessly and bent down to her, powerless to make her stop.

He meshed his hands into her braided hair, pulled that braid apart gently and then pressed her head more to his groin as she pumped and lashed his shaft simultaneously. She craved his inability to keep himself from becoming engulfed by his want of her and of her wanton actions upon him. She felt her own high pitched sexual turmoil as she slowly, then more quickly, ran her fingers into her vault and also caressed her ruby jewel as it throbbed and grew.

Growling and groaning, he managed to speak this, "There are two ships that I am master of. Yes, do that, exactly that!" He found her nipples with a tick of groping as her breasts hung so pendulously, barely above the oak floor. They bobbled with her motion. Just touching her there made his stone hard cock even fuller. He could not believe how she created an exquisite desire within him for her which had to culminate in his powerful release.

His voice was a hoarse whisper and vibrated with sheer need to pour himself past her tongue, down her throat. "These two ships, the Heemskerck and Zeehaen . . . ." His moan was ferocious.

He stammered out the remaining words, "We journey for a long while. No one on ship will serve our hunger. We feed only on nearby coasts, from the sea itself or birds plucked from the sky!"

She was shaking and he was not sure if she had heard or understood him at all. But he was at a point where he truly did not care anymore. Her fist still pounded him top to bottom, her tongue and mouth's pull enveloped him, and she tugged at his nipples as he tugged at hers.

His breath, as he bowed and spoke to her, goaded her into frenzy. She released him from her mouth and still clutching his thick, throbbing length, guided him into her juiced tunnel. She threw her legs around his waist and dug into his ass with her nails drawing tiny trails of blood. His first thrust touched bottom and he became still. He had to feel her sex to the fullest without distraction. Their pulses synchronized and that heightened the ecstasy multifold.

He was no more capable of stopping now than was she. He thrust hard, fast and plumbed her depths. Her flesh gripped his organ in the most devastating of holds and she was crying. Suddenly, she sucked in her breath, clenched her legs around him fiercely, rubbed herself against his groin and dissolved into moans countless times as paroxysms burst rampantly through her core and around his shaft.

Her waves incited his waves of release. He was like a dam crashing; wild and wet over all surfaces. He emptied into her with the seemingly endless soft thuds of his come beating at the back of her vault.

The twitching wire between them had discharged dramatically.

Their heads lolled and neither fancied locating the soon to be departing ships. But they did.

CHAPTER 3

The Heemskerck and Zeehaen

Both Janna and Catrione struggled with the elasticized flatteners that they used to bind their very sizeable breasts to their chests. And Janna had been disgusted with the excessive finery that the Dutch women wore. But now that the pair of them were attempting male disguise, Janna was appalled at what the Dutch men had to endure. Janna and Catrione glanced each other's way and rolled their eyes behind the white powdered, thinly applied clay makeup that thoroughly altered their actual appearance. The powdered wigs did the same for the women's silken manes. All else that they wore was standard male business attire.

Abel and Eumann knew of the unhappiness of their female companions but there was no other option available. The men were privy to the knowledge that any female, let alone two beautiful females, boarding either the Heemskerck or the Zeehaen were a recipe for dissension, discord and disaster. Females did not sail the seas with men. That was forbidden entirely. And then the fights that might break out if Janna and Catrione were discovered. And, if uncontrolled, especially with sumptuously beautiful flesh before them, attempted rape and death, the crews most assuredly, would follow. And having enough sailors to man the ships was critical.

Mutiny was probably the next course of action by the crew to take down the master commander for his gross misjudgment. Again, the crew would fail but lives would be lost and dissention unnecessarily caused. Panic might very well prevail too.

Nightmare upon nightmare would be the order of the day were they to go undisguised!

Janna and Catrione, therefore, had to suffer a smaller torment so as to escape the larger one. And, of course, as vampires all, the four were nearly secure in their power to withstand all harm. Yet why promote violence rather than that of cooperation and a willing spirit?

The women had to find their way onto the Heemskerck, the more warlike of the two vessels. They sauntered towards it in normal fashion so that their presence at later times would appear anything but suspect.

Catrione gazed in awe at the size and sleek look of the vessels before her. The square rigged and three masted yacht with cannon apparent in abundance pleased her no end. She was a strong creature who loved an equally strong partner. And this powerful wood hulk was to be one of her partners now for a very long time. She appreciated that and let herself sink into comfort as her shoes touched the tightly laid wood deck.

Janna walked side by side with her once lost ally and the pair went unnoticed as anything other than traders employed by the Dutch East India Company.

Abel and Eumann did not have to alter their style whatsoever as they strode up to and then into the commander's quarters. Light was hesitating but a minute just before brightening the shadows of late dawn. Eumann followed Abel into the private domain of the superior officer upon these ships. Eumann went as a lesser officer and the disguised women as guests of the master commander.

Abel Tasman, as master commander, was not afraid to dictate terms on these ships. Abel knew better than to be timid with any of those he had charge over.

Besides, there was nothing questionable in that arrangement as far as the sailors were concerned. Many of them were occupied in settling in to their own areas simultaneously and took no notice of the party of mixed officers and business people anyhow.

Though quarters were not shared between Abel and his human associates, two individuals were the key to the success of the journey. They were trusted fully by Abel. He had had to reveal to them his abrupt shift from human to undead. It shocked the navigator, Francois Visscher, and Visscher's assistant, Isaak Gilsemans, to be told the fixed circumstances now but their assent was critical. They had to lead in the bright of daylight while the four demons slept the sleep of the damned. And this Visscher and Gilsemans readily agreed to it. They had worked with Abel before and had absolute confidence in his skills, human or not!

The commander of the second ship, the fluyt Zeehaen, designed to carry cargo back from their exploits, was the talented and capable Ide Holleman. He was equally trusted by Abel and had also been informed of the master commander's transformation. Nothing fazed this individual and he was immediately ready to handle Abel's absence in daylight on the smaller vessel.

As it was, only Visscher and Gilsemans were there to greet Abel as the four vampires rushed into the somewhat cramped room and immediately bolted for the trap door to the bulkhead hold. It was in this hold, snugly below the quarters above, that Abel had tucked four caskets into it during the extreme dark of night as the ship remained docked and the crew was absent and finding rowdy pleasure elsewhere. They had not required caskets, as shelter from the sun was all that was necessary. But this was to be a long journey and he had desired as much comfort for the four of them as possible.

Visscher slammed the trap door closed as the four made haste to their separate enclosures of wood and robust metal. The lids moved smoothly, without creaks or sound at all. The water that sloshed on the outside of the hull was only faintly heard and the very slight motion of the ship from wavelets at ports shore was only comforting. Because of this, dense sleep was brought to them that much faster.

It was August fourteen and all was being prepared for departure. It was to be no later than noon when the tiny flotilla of two was to heave from port and head southwest to the land of Mauritius. This Dutch possession was to then offer Tasman a direct route south into waters and lands basically unknown and not secured by any existent countries.

Proudly, the Dutch standard, the Prince-flag, flew broadly in the mild breeze below the main boom and was visible without a doubt to all water faring folk. This flag carried a red-orange band at the top, a middle white band and then the blue band at the bottom.

Abel's last thought as he swooned into his minds recesses that morning, was how proud he was to have had his own master pick the gentleman and expert sailor, Abel Tasman, to have inhabited this cycle. And he pictured what the reaction of most was when they saw the Dutch emblem flapping elegantly in the wind. The Dutch were considered the supreme navigators and sailors of the time and no wise ships came upon these Dutch fluyts and yachts unless desperate or insane.

Abel suddenly acknowledged pirates. They knew no bounds.

And then complete repose stole him away.

CHAPTER 4

Deception's Dance

Abel had dubbed Janna as Jan, Catrione as Claudios and Eumann as Eugenias for the sake of applying common male Dutch names to their identity. Eumann was not usual amongst the Dutch and so had to go. Janna and Catrione had to have some male name to get them by when the masculine was necessary for them. Names were significant to lull others into the simple notion that they were alike culturally. The vampires shape shifted with their needs easily. Names were not overwhelmingly significant to them in their own right. Name changes were as frequent to them as their thirst for blood was.

Two names that had remained the same were that of Mikilenia the rebel and Anteekwa, his royal consort from a time faded and finished. They had been pursued by Mikilenia's mother, Catrione, and her ever lover, Eumann. And they had been found because Mikilenia had failed to block the vision that Catrione and Eumann used to unearth the pair.

Two hundred years ago, Cahokia Indian brethren had loyally kept pace with the demon and the princess at first leaving but had either gradually dispersed with the passing of time or, for those who had recognized Mikilenia and

Anteekwa as undead, well, they had fled. And traveling alone was no more difficult for the invincible duo than traveling with any flock, large or small. As a matter of fact, for Mikilenia in particular, he had no patience with sorting through group needs, so it was satisfactory when it became simply him and Anteekwa wandering the length and breadth of the North American Continent.

It had never occurred to the couple that his mother actually cared enough for him to make an effort to locate him. Catrione and Eumann had given no indication of concern when Kakeobuk, now Abel, had hostilely attacked Mikilenia and Anteekwa and then had forbidden the two from ever returning to the city of Cahokia. So neither he nor Anteekwa had bothered to block any vampire's vision.

It had been so easy, therefore, for mother and lover to have tracked, located and then confronted the younger couple. They had confronted them with genuine empathy and a conciliatory tone. His mother had no sentiment toward Anteekwa but her rash son was a prize that she truly treasured in spite of a very unfortunate deed having occurred between them so many years ago. The deed had brought punishment to him especially and their anguish over the occurrence was still an occasionally festering sore.

Mikilenia was overwhelmed in his surprise when, after a sublime episode of entwining with beautiful Anteekwa, he peered up out of his erotic haze and found himself locking eyes with his mother's eyes.

Vampire reflexes can be so like human reflexes. Mikilenia froze for a second, gasped deeply and then curled into himself to hide his nudity. Anteekwa recoiled instantly as she sensed her partner's defensive body posture. She did not attempt to cover herself though, she simply hissed at their audience. She had no rapport whatsoever with the two who had been called Ashkipaki and Mahkwa in the far by and by. Even earlier, their original names had been Catrione and Eumann. They had reclaimed those names once grossly disappointed with their experience as Native Americans.

"We are here to offer our urgent sorrow and succor to you, my son. Do not fear us. We wish to renew your hopes and calm your angers."

Brazenly, as what hadn't already been seen before, Mikilenia and Anteekwa stood and dressed in front of the others. Mikilenia, because it was his mother, turned away as he donned his minimal clothing. Anteekwa did not turn away whatsoever. However, she did not link gazes with Eumann, she instead linked gazes with Catrione, as if to say, "My beauty matches yours in every way and may even surpass it."

And Anteekwa, in her pride, did not disturb Catrione whatsoever. She comprehended the marvel that was Anteekwa. Yet she had the confidence in her own superlatives that she waved the boast away and simply assessed Anteekwa's physical luster. As she observed her son's crony, there were many curvaceous similarities between them. It wasn't just the form; it was also the coloration and height that ran parallel, feature to feature. They might have been cousins the likenesses were so uncanny.

It was a given though that Catrione had little respect for Anteekwa. The feeling was returned full force.

So Catrione did not resist reflexively thumbing her nipples very slowly as she studied the Cahokia princess. And her large caramel toned nipples responded fully. Eumann leveled a subtle grin at both women as their silent combat continued.

Eumann was unable to restrain his cock's motion as he scanned both. The heat that rippled his way from the women was unmistakable and rampant. He never would ravish Anteekwa but she was as lush as his wanton partner was. Both had completely flawless skin with sloping breasts that were endless and pendulous. Anteekwa's breasts, because of her greater youth, thrust a bit higher than his lovers. But both women were so huge there. And this on frames that were short and lean. Anteekwa's dark smooth hair complemented her dark smooth thick tips that she squeezed for an instant. The thickness grew and the serpent talisman that hung from her left nipple appeared to take life. She tugged at the copper object once and felt it to her core. She did not make a sound or move a muscle however.

Arousal was truly not on her mind; a signal of warning was at the center of her behavior.

Mikilenia was done and had turned just after Anteekwa had finished her display and had then replaced her several pieces of clothing. It was in that second that Catrione roused herself from her focus upon the scene and took Mikilenia by the arm. He was amused by the gesture but followed his mother as he smiled Anteekwa's way simultaneously. This calmed his love somewhat and she switched her attention to the remaining Eumann. And, since he and Catrione had mapped out their strategy regarding this inevitable encounter beforehand, Eumann happily engaged the lovely young vampire with all vigor. Thorough distraction of Anteekwa was everything in the here and now.

"I am aware that you question my concern for you, Mikilenia. And I have waxed uncertain in times past. Our divide was large those many years ago. But, for me, the divide has narrowed considerably. You are my flesh and blood, my only offspring, and I covet that. I want no harm to come to you ever."

Now began the initiation of deception's dance that was to spiral out in so many unpredictable ways.

Once out of sight and hearing of the smiling Eumann and the serious Anteekwa, Catrione stopped her son and leaned into his ear. She blocked any possible seer probes by Anteekwa that might find the secret that she whispered into Mikilenia's ear. It was a secret that was sure to divide Anteekwa from Mikilenia.

Mikilenia was immediately consumed with the proposal laid out for him. He craved its successful outcome and went to lead his partner upon a path to a new land where the pair was to wait for first European arrival.

It took no time at all for two forms to flit strongly toward the crescent moon and be sucked into the night sky.

Eumann and Catrione then skied in their own direction to Batavia and waters unknown.

CHAPTER 5

Seer Foresight

Mikilenia's moderately developed but still gravely limited capacity of seer foresight led them to the huge slab of land that Catrione had indicated to him existed and existed for her ship to discover soon enough. This was where a confrontation was to take place. Mikilenia wanted his special partner back. He had waited at length for this and was willing to delay a bit more. And he had his lovely Anteekwa to play with in the meantime. None of this thought did he permit to be probed by any other demon, particularly Anteekwa.

They soared over what appeared to be rough terrain. A plume of condensing steam fluffed, curled and then narrowed. The caldera that this superheated tentacle rose from was itself surrounded by the iridescent white of ice upon ice at the summit of a volcano. Flaring from that single smoking pit was a spine of high peaked, snow smothered mountains that ran from one end of the center of the island to the other end. Icy fiords and glaciers were strewn about along the southern coastlines. Lakes pocked the land thoroughly, principally northward. A svelte plain neighboring east and west of the mountainous area was soothing in its green contrast to the cold projected everywhere else below them.

The softness of the plain, near the harbor that his mother had told him of, was their destination. He wanted to bring them to ground rapidly as he had psychically seen Anteekwa's strut with his mother and he was aroused and enflamed to the point where his heartbeat tripped loudly in his bat's chest.

Plentiful grass was mildly crushed beneath their human feet as they contacted soil. Their conversion from bat to human appearance was so instantaneous that feet, rather than claws, touched the matted padding beneath them.

The ever reckless and over confident Mikilenia was swollen and erect in rather mammoth form beneath his breeches before she had even taken her first breath as human. She was a slave to his compulsions though and she felt a surge of wetness lubricate between her thighs with shocking speed. She clenched her thighs even while standing and hugged the elevating pulse as she readied herself for his approach.

A hushed dark skinned female who had gone early to procure firewood for her encampment squatted stock still within the shelter of a dense clump of silver beech trees. Her jaw had dropped and the dark blue tattoos surrounding her lips and upon her chin were distorted in patterns that the pulled and pursed skin created.

Nothing but imminent death would have slowed Mikilenia down in his hunger for his deeply golden companion. He may have found her less than his one true love but she was astounding in her capacity to bring the embers of his sexual flame to an unstoppable whipping fury. Anteekwa's passion for him was at least at his level and more sometimes.

The damp rectangle of flat grass that he had spotted while airborne was sufficient for both of their immediate needs. The chill of the ground's moisture would complement and control the temperature of their skin.

Mikilenia's breathing swooshed out in ragged exhalations as he caressed and cupped her breasts, all the while kissing and sucking at her lips and then her nape. He removed one hand from a linen covered breast of hers and twirled the length of her hair over that hand such that he pulled her head back when he pulled his hand back. He lapped at her forcibly proffered neck, kissed it and grazed it with his fangs. She groped for his few ties that bound his cock beneath his breeches and blindly undid them. With a hand remaining in her hair, he gently directed her head to his now freely expanding organ.

He did not need to direct her in this manner but it was thrilling to her and he knew it. She took his very large instrument and, under the ministrations of her tongue and lips, expanded and lengthened further for her. Her cheeks surrounded his cockhead and puffed visibly out to the side. He loved looking down at her and her up at him when she sucked him heavily. His sweet and clear dew was licked off avidly as she moaned for him and she was unable to keep from closing her eyes periodically and sinking into the vortex of her charged passion.

She could have placed just one hand on his elongated shaft and pumped him rapidly, using her other hand to stroke her own ruby red knob. She loved though pummeling his shaft with both hands as she sucked him intently. So, to directly stimulate herself, she rocked her hips and caused the heel of her foot to apply rhythmic pressure on her opening and clitoris. It was delicious for her.

He let go of her bunched hair and pushed her seeking mouth away from him. He was not ready to come yet and would soon were they to remain with his cock embraced within her mouth.

She trembled as if with palsy as she rushed to remove her final garments.

He laid her nude body down upon the meadows surface and did what he so loved to do to her.

It was what aroused her to where she thrashed, raised her hips and unconsciously swung her cunt slicked flexed thighs apart and then together. This action thrust her crown jewel, hard and throbbing teardrop that it had become, more deeply into his mouth than otherwise would have been feasible. The burn of his mouth's very strong suction upon her nether region and the sensation of his strongly lashing tongue on her clit elevated her pleasure up to hitherto unknown realms.

He had delayed touching her bare breasts just to escalate the build of excitement. But he had to have that now. So, while still seizing her erotic center with his mouth, he raised his arms to her breasts. Bent as he was with his arms spread and extended, he appeared in prayer. And pleasure's prayer was exactly what he and she were involved in.

He pinched, squeezed, twisted and pulled on her so thick raven black right nipple. He mixed these movements up as well. She trembled in the delight of his knowledge, a knowledge that played her so delicately, so skillfully, as only a maestro had the talent to do. And the luxury for them both was when his fingers clasped the metallic object affixed to her left nipple. It was shaped in circular form and he had only to pinch it with thumb and forefinger and then he was able to maneuver her nipple in whatever direction he chose.

The copper serpent spat energy through Mikilenia's fingers and his ardor increased multifold.

He tugged at that object more and more vigorously until Anteekwa was crying in her bliss.

Between gasps, she raised her head up and panted to him, "Take me! Take me hard. Do not be lenient! I need it fast. I need you finding all of me!" She held his face with her hands fiercely.

"Put me inside of you, my love. Do it so that there is no pain. Do it slowly." Mikilenia always feared her pain if gradual dilation was not carefully achieved.

She took his huge erection with both hands and rammed him into her! This time, the fleeting pain was dismissed, and would be evermore, as the stab of his stone hard cock simply acted as a goad for her lust.

He was utterly surprised but felt the stimulation of her abrupt move pierce his loins and heart. He did love her second only to the other. Unless it was the other, Anteekwa remained exclusively prominent in his mind.

And he pounded her so harshly. But her desire enslaved her and permitted his flesh to glide gorgeously against hers. This pummeling of her created a barely felt physical friction but a friction whose magical intensity would soon shatter them both.

Her head jerked upward at the same time that her hips rose in the air. She uttered a guttural and lengthy moan. She held her breath and writhed on his pole as if lightning-struck. The waves split her down her Venus vault's center and she nearly pulled away from him because the feeling became so nearly unbearable in its intensity.

He did not let her go. Instead, he probed her with his entire length, froze there and erupted into his tumultuous release. He was unable to recall pouring more of his liquid into her ever before. Now his cock was lodged to its length and neither he nor she was able to move at all.

This was the Maori female's opportunity to escape. And that she did.

CHAPTER 6

Mauritius Bound

Being Mauritius bound, all on board the Heemskerck and the Zeehaen were informed of the strong possibility that a pirate sloop might sail over the horizon and ominously move towards the weapons laden Dutch ships. Even so, pirates had a method of moving rapidly and lightly in their shallow hulled small craft. The crew of Tasman's vessels had been apprised of further facts that gave severe warning to all regarding the true danger of being confronted by these sea bearing bandits. Even though the waters of the Southern Hemisphere's Atlantic Ocean were not rife with cutthroat bandits, Mauritius was a port in a storm for many of these buccaneers who attempted to avoid capture and arrest. Being out of the way and the last known piece of land in the region that Tasman now traversed made it the perfect hideout for vermin. Yet Tasman had no choice in coming to land there. They had to resupply on this small island. And though he felt fully able to fend off any pirate's incursion, effort's fatigue and the desire to dodge conflict was proving increasingly urgent. Three weeks confined to a bobbing cork in a mass of unpredictable waves was not any of the vampire's dreams of paradise.

Besides, even with the strength of Tasman and his undead comrades, any treasure seeking sloops were a true threat as they usually were only rigged with one mast and were very hard to spot. And also, if there was no wind for their sails, they were small enough craft that they could be rowed just as well. These smaller vessels were packed with guns and were loaded with up to three to four score men. If they approached close enough, they swarmed with the ferocity of creatures hell bent on stealing everything that they could, including the lives of the innocent victims. They rarely left any captives alive after interrogation. First came questions asked, then torture and then came death. It was ghastly cruelty and torment beyond the imagining.

Dusk was fast approaching this one afternoon but, as it turned out, not approaching fast enough. Tasman, Janna, Eumann and Catrione were all pinned to their caskets in the anesthesia of the demon. The rest of the two crews were just exchanging day to evening stints and were malingering a bit as they exchanged boasts and flurries of conversation one to the other.

A single mast suddenly flared into view between the fluyt and the yacht. Canon shot was fired over one Dutch bow and one Dutch boom as warning; no pirate chose to see his booty sink to the ocean floor. The Dutch crews froze in place as the Dutch sails were peppered with small shot. Men on board scattered and gave way to the musket bullets slamming into their decks.

Some of Tasman's sailors were struck down immediately while others fled below decks. There were those daring few who attempted to man the weapons and fire upon the criminal hoard. But it was too late and they were easy targets who were shot dead before they were even able to place hands to cannons.

The screams of the dying blended with the raging calls of the boarding pirates created a cacophony of sounds that was so piercing and terrible it even penetrated the sleep-locked minds of those who began to rouse with the setting sun.

The four moved with great and sudden wrath. They did not hesitate and the murderous onslaught was over in minutes.

What the vampires came upon was a bloodied deck with twisted and broken dead bodies and with the survivors cowering before garishly clothed, bearded brawny men. These men had scimitar-like cutlasses poised to be brought down upon some of the Dutch crew's heads. There was an obvious leader who screamed in triumph and shouted commands to his hodgepodge of maniac raiders. His hair seemed to surround his face in long tangled black locks with a full and unkempt beard and a mustache that made his upper lip vanish. The glee that sparked from his eyes was instantly obvious and called the vampires like a beacon.

Tasman led but they all moved so swiftly that a susurration through the air was all that was apparent. Even that was so marginal that it did not register until after the fact that it had been real. And it had been very real. The pirates, had they lived, would have sworn on their own watery graves that it was the harshest of reality.

The last act of the hirsute leader of these vicious buccaneers was that of attempting to make the near corpse before him eat his own lips. The shiny red blood that was splashed upon the cutlass blade attested to the fact that these lips had just been sheared from the groveling and crumpled man's face. The pirate snapped the man's head back and all were capable of hearing the crack of the sailor's neck. It was at that instant of jamming the lips into the mouth and slamming the face to the wood deck that the villain reaped his reward and paid the price of his astounding cruelty.

The consequences of the blurred and nearly invisible motion was astounding as the brute captain's head stilled for but a flash, the light in his eyes dimmed and died in disbelief as he fell torso first and his now eternally silenced head flew to a distance with crushed carotid and a crimson stream draining from the hideously dismembered appendage.

This carnage was repeated over and over until none of the assailants remained; whereupon the four flashed to their hold below the master commander's quarters and then revisited the scene as the people all the others believed them to be.

The number of savaged crew on both ships amounted to approximately one third of the original number. Abel was devastated as were Janna, Eumann and Catrione.

The headless bodies and the once attached heads were treated with disgust and disdain and were tossed over the side without as much as an after look. Their Dutch compatriots all were wrapped in plain cloth with stone weights attached, a few words spoken and then they were slid over the rail into the sea. This was done in the dark of night as reaching the shores of Mauritius was even more paramount after the attack. Their store of supplies was not all that required replenishment; they also had to find more bodies to assist in the continuation of their journey.

The rumors that passed magically to Mauritius told of mysterious actions against pirates that would eventually reach legendary status. Any pirates on shore who had a notion of dubiously treating Abel or his men were quickly squashed. Abel found that he was approached courteously and his needs were efficiently tended to.

Ship supplies were restored and some capable and some not so capable men were found for the journey ahead. There was little choice and so they sailed away with what they managed to obtain.

In the truly vast and unknown waters that their two ships now plied, there would be no random attacks as they had just experienced. Pirates did not exist there.

If not pirates, what then?

CHAPTER 7

Propitious Opportunity

Four caskets in a small hold with two others at no more than arm's length away provided almost no propitious opportunity for lover's lovemaking. It was not Catrione who insisted upon privacy for their intimacies but rather Eumann who wished for her passion sounds to be unfettered and openly heated. How was that to be accomplished when self-consciousness of others presence inhibited all action? Strangely, privacy and embarrassment were aspects of the tableau of feeling these creatures labored under.

And besides, she had to always pose as Claudios when on the deck. How seemly would it have been for this Claudios to be seen embracing Eugenias. Male to male displays of affection or more were despised by any and all onboard. It brought immediate discipline or ruthless immediate violence against the perpetrator.

Her burden grew as she acted the masculine role. It drove her wild but she understood the sheer necessity of it.

Catrione had been wet for Eumann throughout this sea passage. She was the most sexually starved of the two always. Her juices were forever flowing and her urges were always unbridled. It was Eumann who had to act to tame her impulses. Yet that never stopped her throb for him from occurring. And that throb, at its least was hard pounding and at its most was ready to burst into release.

She was so sensitive every minute of every night. Her only relief was in the day where sleep was demanded. He could touch her skin anywhere, whisper in her ear, kiss her lips tenderly and, oh my, were he to brazenly cup a breast from behind in an instant of his desire, her core of passion melted into a contraction of dense energy that then expanded forcefully into burning tentacles radiating into her stiffened nipples, bright red and expanded jewel and a delectably itching vaginal interior. She was filled deliciously with erotic fervor, so much so that she wondered how she did not come over and over simply from the touch of salty air upon her flesh.

Even when she had put fingers to his concavity of form at right ankle where he had bitten a chunk of his own flesh from his bone and spit it forcefully away, she nearly swooned in desire for him. That revoltingly disfigured area of his reminded her of his torment from the busy fleas constantly probing his absent flesh there. That itching had nearly driven him mad until he had torn the offending skin from his ankle with his teeth and left it, and the fleas, to waste away in one of the misbegotten and barren lands that they had scoured in search of her son those many years ago. And that very ugly portion of his body, even that ignited her passion for him. It roused her greatest maybe. It was, after all, his badge of bravery that he suffered any pain and action to right what was otherwise twisted.

It was several hours only before dawn when the ships were to depart Mauritius.

She had to do this. She would not insist. She would simply take him as land provided what sea had not.

She took her Eumann by the hand and psychically instructed him to fly with her to an oasis of expansive white sands beach. It was undiscovered and they would not be disturbed in what was to be her feast of him.

Once upon the cooling sands of the early morning, the clothing of Claudios was shed to reveal a radiant and gorgeous Catrione beneath. Eugenias stripped himself of his clothing too and Eumann, as ever, was thrilled. She was a marvel of beauty and he never tired of it. As a matter of fact, as he understood her effort in restraining herself when locked to the Heemskerck, he prized her more and more. Her grace was equally stunning with the beauty that she carried so naturally.

Standing absolutely nude before him, Catrione swayed subtly and let her hands ride down the long slopes of her breasts until she was cupping each and using her thumbs to stroke her lavish and lengthening nipples. There was urgency in his approach to her as he nudged one of her thumbs away with his closed mouth and then opened his lips and sucked hard on the one tip. She tilted her head slightly backwards, let her hair fall away from her body, closed her eyes, moaned in a barely bridled lusty satisfaction and, with torso and hands, shoved her bounty further into his mouth. She tugged on the back of his head with both hands so that the message was unmistakable.

It was not so much the sweet taste and warm feel of her thick caramel tip that he sucked on forcefully, tongue lashing it back and forth that heightened his longing but instead was what he wrought regarding Catrione's fervor. She was at a fever pitch to begin and every goading touch of his, no matter how soft or demanding, prompted her to make sounds and motions that created eagerness in him for her.

He bathed in the fact that she was short in stature and singularly heavy in breast. She and Janna were huge in that regard except that Janna was tall and with hair coloring that was blond favoring auburn. His Catrione was short and she had nary a trace of blond in her hair coloring; it was dark as a raven's coat. But those were trifles in comparison to the drape of her breasts upon her chest. And miraculously, the very pendulous fall of her mounds did not alter their youthful thrust. Gravity was defied and Eumann was more than grateful that his love for her was additionally sparked by this fact.

And now that spark had developed as a profoundly searing feeling in his very swollen cock.

She reached down for his size and gasped as she released it from his breeches. She too never had enough of his massive love for her.

It was then that Eumann parted from Catrione's breast and softly, assuredly, laid her down upon the sands beneath them.

She placed her hands above her head and clasped her wrists tightly. She spread her legs widely and wantonly.

"I am your captive my love. Though I am not restrained, I am restrained. My hands are tied and I cannot move them." She panted after she spoke.

He kissed her over and over so that her panting escalated and found a more rapid rhythm. His breathing had a ragged quality to it as well and his heart pounded and made him light headed in his need for her.

Her intentions of not moving her arms dissolved.

With eyes closed, she found and fondled his thick shaft. She had to; she imagined his dew and had to. And it was there. She swirled the delicate liquid all over his cockhead. And then she encircled his pulsing cap with thumb and forefinger and rubbed it up and down rapidly over his flaring shape. She firmed the circle up and then loosened it. She felt the enlargement and tightness of his length as she did this. Then she gripped his column and pumped him in a frenzy.

Eumann was deeply stirred by her actions. He was nearing his threshold and was stunned that he was about to be first to reach his climax. She felt the greater broadening of an already thick and long instrument and she comprehended that his release was imminent. So she held him off as she craved a simultaneous explosion.

She guided his jerking shaft to her Venus vault and she held it at her entrance. Her wetness was copious now. She almost did not sense him when she rubbed his plum colored cap over her jewel and opening. The natural lubricants were almost too much. So she decided to plunge him into her.

Then she felt the intensity of their contact. He had growled when she had forced him all the way into her. He froze an instant and luxuriated in her complete depths.

It was when he froze, before he began to pound her hard, that the feeling of their connection enveloped her. She writhed on his pole and she placed one palm on his chest and squeezed his sensitive nipple with the other as he thrust over and over. The sand that she moved upon acted to invigorate her more.

She was blinded, smote down, by the crashing of her own ecstatic waves as they found a beat that followed the beat of the cresting and crashing ocean waves at shoreline.

He was simultaneously hypnotized and was utterly wracked by her spasms rippling upon his livid cock and his release pummeled her insides with a wash of pounding hot liquid that repeated until he felt as if he were forever emptied.

She was full, so full. His pearlescent load seeped from around his shaft and out to meet her thighs and then the bed of sand underneath them.

Leaving that spot was the most difficult thing to do. But they had to.

They joined Abel and Janna as all settled into their caskets.

Orb's rays reached for them then but were too late.

CHAPTER 8

Van Diemen's Land

This bastard crew was a miracle of efficiency and capability. Abel was dumbstruck with his luck! He might just visit Mauritius more frequently and lure men aboard to provide future muscle and compliance. They had already moved south below the forty ninth latitude and were now clipping the waves at breakneck speed along the forty fifth latitude, plying east. He would only use his seer sight if absolutely necessary as he felt the thrill, and episodic chill, of barging into vast expanses of hitherto unknown, never before traversed sea.

By god this was mighty to feel!

He was elated and sensed himself to be truly invincible. The huge expanse of dark blue water, the smashing sound of waves slashed in two, the hissing of wave drenching, whipping liquid that surged over the Heemskerck's side was a testament to his master and his master's power and strength. He and his master clashed often but this was not one of those moments. The entity found himself invigorated by the elemental challenges that were being blithely thrown his way; this was one of those rare gifts that his one and only superior authority bestowed upon him which stirred his undead blood. He was commander and was joyful at the opportunity to seize the ocean currents and become lord over all that was visible.

Janna embraced him from behind and felt his thrill at the sting of saltwater pellets lashing at his face. She was always captivated when his wonder at the miracle of the world dampened his primitive appetites; his bloodlust. Her thirst was never as vast as his was yet hers existed and she was always ashamed of the dominance of those primal undead urges.

She had thirsted for love, not the entity's then, and that had led her onto the path of the demons that strode in the rank gloom of dark only. Love had done this to her! And then that love had deserted her. Her pain and anguish had been vast then and the hurt was only assuaged by her later discovery of the increasingly gentled entity. It was he that she burned hot for now and it was a heat that was incessant and seemingly limitless.

She sensed him always but had to read him with concentration and all of her seer powers that she had managed to muster in her time as vampire before she was able to precisely locate him within the skin that he had fundamentally taken over. And even then, it was only with his permission that she found him there. And he let her in rather easily. He loved her equally to the same degree that she loved him. So he assented to have her link in to Abel's most amorphous parts, the parts that were his core and that made his power manifest.

It had taken a bit of time and seer effort before she understood how her entity shared this present skin with Abel. The entity vibrated within the vehicle that was Abel's human form. But Abel was there as well. The simplest way to put it, Janna realized, was to conjure up the easy notion of dominance and submission. The entity dominated and Abel submitted. Abel submitted without resistance either. Abel's human spirit observed and occasionally laid its opinion on the dominant other. This was only done when necessity was imminent, alarming and the cursed spirit was on the verge of running amuck.

The only other responsibility that Abel's soul, Janna called it that for want of a better word, had, other than to watch and rarely restrain the other, was to take over Abel's skin once that skin had been abandoned by the black creature at the command of his master.

Janna was so deep into her thoughts and the comforting sensation of her closeness to Abel that she failed to hear the approach of several additional individuals. Eumann and Catrione were two of the small cluster that sought Abel and Janna's' company. Abel's seconds on the Heemskerck, Visscher and Gilsemans, ambled up to the prow to offer opinions to their master commander. Unfortunately, several lesser of the crew had been curious in addition. What was the slight commotion occurring and why was the head of this expedition poised and alert? Yet they lagged a bit.

It was this lag that allowed Janna to release her embrace of Abel and then to stand stiffly as if she were Jan, male, and simply finding fascination in Abel's fascination. It also helped greatly that she had been wise enough to dress her part too. Catrione, as Claudios, had done the same.

And as the laggards arrived, their curiosity at Abel's tense concentration grew. What was it?

Abel told them but only turned his head to them as he pretended to use the light of the beaming moon to have illuminated his discovery. As a vampire, he had seen shore himself but had to act otherwise to fool those ignorant of his true status.

He pointed with straight and extended arm to a mass of rocks that formed a perimeter surrounding the remnants of an upward sloping beach ending in thick forested trees. Land had been found but not quite breeched yet.

Again, the eyes of the uninformed forced the four undead to restrain themselves. They were no more capable of flying to this shore than they were capable of releasing their fangs and driving them into carotids of any of their crew members.

The necessary pretense was maddening for Abel, Janna, Eumann and Catrione.

Visscher was eager to plant the Dutch flag upon this heretofore undiscovered ground and claim it for his mother country. But he knew that the ship was not small enough to avoid the rocks circling the land. Even the Zeehaen was not small enough to ply its way through what was a set of rocky teeth that did not yield to ships at all.

Visscher was not at all eager himself to do the honors of which he was so adamantly enamored. He did not know how to swim and would not have regardless. The waves slapped at the ship's hull without letup. And he was aware that even the most agile and strong of swimmers might drown before reaching the shore's safety. Was a flag worth that? Not by him! Visscher would not ease up on Abel though. He insisted that it had to be done!

Abel turned fully then and signaled Eugenias to step forward. He did without flinching. He was never one to fear anything except the loss of his partner. That was the one and only fear that lay dormant in his monster's heart.

"I will perform exactly as you wish, Abel. Where is the flag? If no one has one I will go and fetch one."

"No one has one," retorted Abel.

Eugenias disappeared into the shadows.

"What shall we call this land, Commander?" Gilsemans wondered.

Visscher inserted himself into the discussion again. Abel accepted the man's brashness here as he was not replaceable. So Abel overlooked the annoyances that Visscher occasionally prompted in him. "Our backers for this trek are led by Van Diemen. Logically, it should be called Van Diemen's Land."

"That is what it will be called then." Abel closed that issue quickly.

CHAPTER 9

Predator and Prey

The shadow of upper grey, then slate white underbelly and black fin of Carcharodon carcharias swirled in larger and larger circles, hurtling along at a dozen miles per hour through the inky blue depths of the temperate waters. All senses were at the ready as hunger was pinging from belly to mind without relief. His forty five hundred pound bulk and seventeen foot length glided swiftly through the salty liquid with every sense sharply attuned.

His magnificent brain coordinated all the complex, discrete senses that he possessed to locate and eliminate his prey. His massive snout and the two forward facing nostrils allowed water to flow through these passages of his. Abundant cells lining the folds of skin within these passages alerted him immediately to odors and blood within a pool size area. He detected nothing out of the ordinary presently.

These nasal cavities of his also gave him the capacity to smell out direction. He smelled nothing out of his left cavity and so did not swerve left. He also smelled nothing out of his right cavity and so did not swerve right. With this information, he slowed and now maintained a circular motion. He kept slowing as he began to anticipate something probably imminent.

He heard certain unusual scraping sounds that stopped his motion completely. Only his tail fin swung slowly side to side simply for balance. He began to prepare himself and became poised in position. Was it a distress sound that he heard? His primitive but lethal and highly meshed set of impressions did not indicate that any creature was in distress nearby. He let his eyes inform him of objects within his wide field of view. And there was an enormous ridge of wood that became visible suddenly. The sounds were the anchor as it moved slightly over submerged terrain.

His hunger, but also his enormous curiosity, caused him to wave his tail faster and to cautiously thrust him forward toward this alien object. The size of it made him retreat a bit. His hearing brought sounds of surface waves forcefully slapping at the hull's curvature. The ocean beast had never before encountered something of such a strange nature. He held his body taut now and dove deeper for more watery protection. Even this violent monster was capable of nervous hesitation. But he was also caught in the web of hunger and curiosity that would not let him depart.

He did keep his mouth slightly open; his serrated rows of teeth and very active taste buds were at the ready therefore. If he had been able to salivate, he would have been doing that copiously. He had a large belly to fill and he was forever reminded of this by abdominal signals that seemed to never cease. He did not know the feeling of satiation. It was not a state that he was ever permitted.

The subtlest of his capacities for killing were his electroreception and lateral line. Something in his neighboring waters had just clanged within his nerve endings. A rush of nerve impulses from the ampullas situated in his head shot to pores on his skin surface via jelly-filled tubes and he felt the electromagnetic field of an object that had just crashed through the water's surface and was moving rapidly towards him. A second set of tubes, running up both of his sides, tucked just under his skin and lined with finely weaving hair-like protuberances, also whiplashed him. He froze as his anticipation grew fiercely. The water within this lateral line was fluctuating in a back and forth pattern and he knew that some about to be swallowed creature was approaching him.

His appetite was to be sated in an instant or two more.

To accelerate the process, as his belly hard hammered him now, he flapped his huge tail and tore into the fleshy object at his snout. His black doll eyes rolled back and became white; this white was as lifeless in appearance as was the black. Nothing else was lifeless within him though.

Blood gushed from the body and its patterns created crimson puffs and threads which hung delicately in the minimally moving underwater currents. It was then that the thrashing began to commence and the water was churned into a frenzy of bubbles, torn chunks of flesh and long gleaming teeth which shredded everything in its path.

The cartilaginous skeleton of the finned behemoth shimmied and shook in the much more difficult encounter than had been anticipated. His brain was accustomed to submission of prey at the instant that his jagged rows of teeth clamped onto flesh of another fish. This was no fish though. And there was no submission here.

Ragged wounds were inflicted and one shape was stunned and without motion suddenly. The initial blast of pain experienced circled inward and began to shut down all conscious function. Then it heaved and was hungry no more as it began to slowly sink into the depths, gathering speed as it generated less and less resistance to the downward pressure of its now watery grave. Just before it disappeared from sight, Eugenias retrieved the flag that he had plunged into the shark's eye.

That gathering of the flag back to his bosom was necessary as the entire reason for his flight into the cold and unconcerned water was to plant this wood shaft with rectangular material mounted on its upper half in Dutch colors on shore for all to see.

Once he had jumped over the ships rail into the ocean, he had been so preoccupied that he had not been alert to the Great White shark that had neatly blended into the hues of the rocky ocean floor. His natural instinct once confronted though was to viciously drive the slender stake of the flag into the most vulnerable area of the fish. And the soft flesh at the shark's eye yielded exactly as Eugenias had expected. All coordination had vanished in an instant because the spike penetrated into the brain as well. And then the predator became the prey and Eugenias simply used his fangs and ripped the boneless body into many pieces.

It was an awesome outcome in that the overlord of the sea had been overcome in such an efficient and easy manner. Was there not a creature alive that was able to do in the demon vampire? It seemed not and Eugenias' ability to defy all attackers, large and small, was astonishing. He was fully aware that any of his vampire companions could also have done the same.

He raised his head above the waves and continued swimming toward the raised soil beckoning him. He swam as if he were human so that all human eyes registered that fact. It made his task that much more difficult as he so desired simply to fly to the mysterious land.

Finally, after what seemed like hours to Eugenias, he planted his toes into sand while the water lapped at his shins and then he left the water altogether and felt the dense yet giving feel of the cooling sands beneath both of his feet.

What he would have given to explore this lush forest that sheltered itself at the edge of the pristine beach. But, again, that was impossible and he would not reveal himself for what he truly was.

So, instead, he found a tall fir tree that stood insolently alone on an outcropping which had outlasted the tides for years. He punctured the ground with the flagpole; he watched it for moments as it flicked and snapped in the potent breeze then gusting. He made sure that the Dutch colors held proudly to the wind and he was satisfied that this territory was now claimed for Holland in perpetuity.

He scanned the foamy and cruel appearing white caps before he ventured into the waves again. He used his seer sight and scanned his path back to the ship. It was to be a much easier project this time than last. The waters were no longer fraught with savage beasts now that the Great White was permanently disposed of.

He stroked smoothly until he found rope dangling from the side of the Heemskerck. His triceps and his calf muscles bulged as he hefted himself up and over the wood rail that he had rashly jumped over earlier. He had done this for Abel's sake and none other. It would not have befitted the rank of Master Commander to have had Able do the deed.

Abel slapped him on his shoulder, wrapped his arm around Eugenias' face, clasped a palm of one hand to the fist of his other and then pulled him nearly nose to nose. "You have done well. Always my thanks to you."

Eugenias shrugged it off.

As inferior to his superior, it was simply required.

Chapter 10

War's Brutality

Abel's entire body appeared so tightly clenched that Visscher swore he felt a fist of heat punch out of his Master Commander's form. Tasman held his hands tightly to his skull with eyes squeezed closed and his lips buckling in on one another. He trembled because he pulled his muscles so tautly to himself. The navigator knew enough to withhold interruption of any kind.

The entity within Abel was concentrating so intently because he desired to force his seer power further forward in time than he had managed in his past. He understood that they were rapidly approaching land and he was determined to find what they were to encounter as he planned on landing ashore. It had not been that way off the newly anointed Van Diemen's Land but it was to be that way at next sight of shore.

Images began to gel for Abel and they were glimpses, and then stark views, of war's brutality. The impact on Abel was immediate and made the being within flinch but go forward anyhow. To imagine himself as anything but impervious to human hardship was inconceivable. He so fooled himself more and more often.

He first perceived a tableau that was startling in its obvious reflexive nature for the individuals involved. The females in this scene of his were well at the margins of any and all activity here. From the maw of a hilltop wood fortress, a small number of dark skinned males, tall and broad of torso, silently flowed down the slope to level ground. This was certainly a war party and they were led by an even brawnier male in large cloak wrapped over his shoulders and a thick leather hide around the waist which served to hold a stone knife blade hanging at the hip. The cloak he wore singularly. All the rest had not only these knifes tucked into their belts but they all carried wooden clubs in one hand and a long plain wooden spear, sharp tipped, in their other hand.

Their stealth impressed Abel. This was not an open attack for sure. The silence of surprise hung on these men as clearly as a perfect diamond was clear.

The lengthy black and wavy hair fell to their shoulders and the tattoos on their faces were vividly evident as they had no facial hair. Their lips were pulled back in a rictus and their gleaming white teeth showed through the grimaces on their faces. Brown eyes were bent to the terrain in order to find their way quickly and quietly. Their thick and muscled legs carried them to that purpose; swiftly and with the muscularity to step carefully.

It was several hours before dawn and this lent potency to their ambuscade as the enemy certainly was asleep and ill prepared for attack. Woe to that enemy, whoever they might be, as Abel recognized that massacre was on the minds of these warriors and there was to be no give in this encounter. Mana had been disturbed and it was time for that infraction to be countered and corrected. Avenging their honor was paramount and unrelenting.

As they reached the perimeter of the hapless village before them, they hunched down and awaited the ideal moment for attack. Their leader was about to give the signal for pitched assault when they themselves were surprised; and were surrounded by those that they sought to annihilate. Long spears flashed through the air. They were unable to retreat as they were certain to face the very clubs that they had readied only moments ago. And, surely, if they advanced upon the village, the villagers were poised and anticipating their approach. What intelligence had leaked from the first war party to the second? Abel did not know. Had they simply been vigilant as Abel sensed that fighting occurred frequently among these people? Preparedness at all times must have been the key to these people's successful existence.

Regardless, Abel heard the terrifying shouts and the clash of spears and clubs. The spear was thrown by some but the remainder held their spears and used them to thrust the razor sharp tips at their foe. If they managed to wound another at a distance after flinging a spear, then they would club and gut their opponent with a quick upward slash of the knives at close quarters. The motion had to be rapid and sure handed. One opportunity was all that was usually presented.

Victims were stabbed, speared and clubbed from behind as well. And, though the original aggressors were greater in number than the men of the small village, the shock of being encircled caused fear and dread within them. Their hapu was cut down to vastly reduced dimensions in quick time. And the carnage was merciless. The fallen group's members were dead or wounded. The wounded were immediately sent to their maker with a knife stroke to the throat. Bloody gashes that spurted blood dotted the scene thoroughly.

The few wounded that were least injured and able to move on their own were promptly tethered together and walked to the settlement that had escaped their own devastation. They became slaves to their conquerors.

This was grisly enough for Abel but there was more.

The least savaged bodies of the dead enemy were dragged back through the stockade door of the fortification upon the hill. It seemed that this pa was a standard and repeated structure of protection for each cluster of these people. Abel surmised that and understood the necessity with such a violent people.

His greatest alarm, and the entity had seen much in his long span of existence, came at the butchering and eating of these dead bodies. Nothing was spared. The corpses were disemboweled, then further cut up with obsidian flake knives and flesh was cooked on heated stones laid in pits in the ground. Organs were fully consumed without leaving a trace; the brain was considered a delicacy and the honor of eating that body part went to the chieftain.

In addition, he scanned intensively enough that he figured one further trait of these natives. It revealed their lack of waste of any kind. They had a storehouse of human meat scraped from the bone and dried in order that future war parties had food that was simple to transport in pouches, baskets or potted in fat in gourds and was equally easy to eat. His scanning exposed the fact that they also put human bone to use in many practical and decorative ways. Flutes were created from it; they used bone as the heads of bird spears, as fish hooks and as rings for captive parrots. Pins and needles were made from human bone. The entity was aghast. He observed human heads and skulls to be used in games of recreation. Or they were simply impaled on a spike above the wooden walls of their stockade to frighten others away.

The entity was aware that Janna knew all of this within the instant of his cognition. He felt her focus upon him and his psychic journey through the war torn land. He understood that she was adamant about not judging these beings. He and she rent flesh on a daily basis.

Yet he still sneered at the islanders' image because vampires did not ever defile one another. Some boundaries were sacred.

Abel released his hand from his head and softened his tense posture. Visscher was greatly relieved that Tasman was finding a relaxed stance again and that whatever had captured his attention was now past.

Janna, on the other hand, recognized precisely what they were to face upon next landing.

CHAPTER 11

Coiled Snake

Abel had quit the vision of the warfare and cannibalism of the natives about to be encountered. Janna, on the other hand, had not. And what exposed itself to her were the despicable forms of Mikilenia and Anteekwa gathered above the collected members of the village just successful in their conflict. How were they here?

It appeared to her that the rebel undead and his whore mistress were the intelligence leak that brought about a satisfactory ending for these humans. And it also appeared to her that an alliance had been established and settled between the undead two and the natives who sat in rapt attention at the feet of her own enemy.

Her surmise was that Mikilenia and Anteekwa would have saved their allies if those selfsame allies had not been able to vanquish their foe on their own.

It was the next sequence of events that Janna pictured that forced her to grip Abel's sleeve. He had been about to walk away in hushed conversation with his navigator were it not for Janna's exclamation to him. "They are near us!"

Abel heard the urgency in her voice and jerked his head towards her. "Who is near us?"

"It's the pair who you banished so many years ago at Cahokia. And they are mounting an alliance; probably an alliance that will eventually conspire against us. Look to it my love! Refocus!"

Abel followed her thread instantly which saved him the effort of losing seconds gathering his seer vision again. And what they both saw appalled but did not surprise them. Should they interfere or should they delay? Abel stood head and shoulders above the duo in power and so was unconcerned. At least, he was unconcerned enough to postpone interference. He wanted to watch what was to transpire. Janna did not have the power to interfere; only Abel did. So she stood stock still with her lover while they both witnessed the spectacle.

Collectively, the theater of their minds watched the two errant undead as Mikilenia and Anteekwa cast themselves into a ceremony with the victorious natives. Several nights had passed since the corpses of the defeated hapu had been piled up and then been feverishly reduced to nothing. No decimated bodies were in sight as the fires of the fortress lit the midnight sky.

Mikilenia and Anteekwa stood silently above the rest and swayed to the rhythmic chant uttered from a multitude of mouths. The crackling fire brought warmth that allowed the entire male throng to have gone bare chested. The women wore their flaxen cloaks uniformly tied over the right shoulder. All sat except the standing two who wore what appeared to be the traditional garb of this, and maybe every, tribe. Mikilenia had nothing on above his waist and his strong and gleaming torso showed easily in the snapping and altering light of the flame. He wore a woven garment that was belted and fell to his knees only. His feet were fully uncovered. This is how the remaining males were garbed as well. Anteekwa mirrored the women surrounding her and had flung over her ample chest the cloak and the skirt that slid comfortably to her lower thighs.

There was a thick plaited mat that each couple, and they all formed couples it appeared to the seer sighted, had brought to this gathering. The largest and most supple mat of all lay at the feet of the swaying pair.

The chant seemed to mesmerize and hypnotize the crowd. The bodies of the native audience moved in perfect swaying unison that now met the motion of the lovely two standing before them. Expectation and anticipation were sizzling in the clarity of that energy.

The male undead suddenly spoke in the language of these people, "We make a covenant with you in the shadows of your powerful fire. Allow us to share our gifts with you to reveal our desire to be one with you. And make no mistake, our gifts are captivating and beyond what you have experienced before. Our power in all things makes the power of the flame dwindle into an orange speck. She and I are mighty. Let us make a union of our collective strengths!"

Oh how the entity regretted sharing his gift with them as well.

Anteekwa led by saying, "We build you."

The group responded by intoning over and over, "You build us."

Mikilenia turned to his partner and smiled wickedly her way. "Show your beauty my wondrous creature. Reveal yourself to them now. Let them truly build!"

Anteekwa was unique among the women gathered in that she was petite, even tiny. The other women rose above her in their height. And those native women were sumptuous in their curves but no one had ever seen the curves that Anteekwa possessed. And so they gasped as she worked to disengage her clasp at right shoulder and Mikilenia, in his impatience, lifted her cloak with a three foot spear. The knife point came close to her fragile skin but did not touch it. Instead, he lifted the cloak slowly and let her breasts fall heavily and bobble for moments. It was immediately after this display that she flung the cloak from herself.

Even Abel and Janna panted in the escalating excitement.

Visscher had long ago retreated to his quarters as he had not been invited into their present domain.

The objects of the crowd's lust stepped onto their mat. The other couples did the same. The flames seemed to flicker and spark more so than before. A storm of erotic happenings was on the brink. They would all be enveloped soon.

There was a labored hush as the copper talisman seemed to hiss. It was a tiny circular ornament that had the head of a coiled snake looming in its center. Her dark and thick nipples grew long and fat; the eyes upon her made her throb beyond her imagining. She was unable to resist tugging on her talisman over and over. She moaned each time that she stretched her nipple in that manner. And she swayed some more.

Mikilenia took his belt and loosened it so that he could remove his only item of clothing. His cock was monstrous in its size and brilliant in its color. His cockhead almost took on the purple hue of the ripened plum. His shaft was a vivid and hot red. His side veins were starkly blue and the pulse there swished again and again.

All the pairs watching mimicked the removal of clothing. Only the women had on their belted garments.

Abel and Janna even felt their breaths intensifying. They were alone and Abel stroked Janna's nipples through her disguise. She was unable to resist Abel in spite of her resistance to anything that involved Mikilenia.

"This serpent is our god of fertility. Let it join with yours and create so much good fortune for your generations to come." Mikilenia spoke.

The entranced pairs muttered together, "Ahhhhhhhhhh" and nodded hypnotically up and down. They were all tethered and paid no attention to anything else.

The rebel stroked his thick tool slowly. Clear dew oozed from his bulbous head. Anteekwa gazed at his organ and leaned into his cock. Her mouth barely engulfed its size and then she lashed it with her tongue. She loved the taste of his flesh and dew. His cockhead swelled even further under her ministrations. They heard collective moans interspersed with gasps from the villagers.

He lifted her woven skirt and sank his fingers into her liquid opening. Anteekwa quailed at this thrust and ripped that skirt from around her waist. He had gone down to his knees panting and growling in pleasure. He removed those fingers of his and spread her lips. He sucked ravenously on her bright red jewel. She was so excited that the hood of her clitoris had receded completely. Her jewel was large and exposed as a tiny penis would be. He had been unable to resist its heat and appearance.

She threw her head back; her luscious long raven hair touched her buttocks. Her very pendulous and gorgeous breasts were inadvertently pushed out for all to see in every detail. Her vast curves mounded erotically and her black nipples jutted hugely. The talisman seemed to grow of its own accord. The serpent was ready to strike and make all propitious.

The couples were writhing on their mats after all the women had been completely disrobed. The men waited to enter their partners upon Mikilenia's unspoken signal.

That came now. He laid his paramour down and told her to close her eyes and spread her limbs as widely as possible. He touched her opening with his instrument. He didn't enter just yet. "You must beg. Beg for it. Do it now!"

"Please, oh god please! Fill me! You must!" Her hips rose to his cock. He thrust himself into her absolute depth. She shivered in desire.

Their audience followed identically.

And when his cock felt her velvet glove, he went wild. He hard pounded her thoroughly. Her pelvis vibrated from his strokes. It went straight to her center. Her jewel blossomed then into a wave of heat that rippled throughout her and then exploded back to her center and out from that core. Anteekwa burned in the tidal heat and was swathed fully; it was completely out of her control. She bucked beautifully in release; waves and waves of it. As soon as Mikilenia felt this, his cock jerked his pearly ejaculate into her. His spurts paralyzed him and he growled and moaned in the utmost pleasure.

All others were absorbed and finding their pathway to bliss. Interior spurts and simultaneous craven moans, then groans, occurred.

Abel and Janna swooned into one another's arms. They forced themselves to wait though.

CHAPTER 12

Ships of Sail

As soon as he released his ejaculate into Anteekwa, he felt the prick of Abel and Janna's seer sight. He mustered his screen against this and felt frustrated that he had not been more vigilant. He had known that they were close. Why had he not shielded himself throughout? Passion weakened him as he failed to concentrate fully on the psychic darts of his enemy.

He whispered in Anteekwa's ear gently as they briefly languished on their mat. "Guard yourself love. You are being observed. I have been too. Use your ability now and keep them out!"

She whispered, "Yes!" The word came out of her mouth in a harsh style as she was very frustrated with herself.

"That same revelation came to me just before you spoke. My passion overcame me. It will not happen again!"

Janna and Abel blinked as their kaleidoscope of images vanished. A heavy black shine totally obscured any further visibility of Mikilenia and Anteekwa. This had been bound to happen. Most vampires were typically very cautious regarding any intrusion upon their thoughts.

The Master Commander and his disguised companion had all the information that was necessary anyhow. They had a taste of the people and the influence of their foe upon these people.

With assurance of their secrecy restored, the rebel and his consort went their way to find their protection from the light of day. It would be the next eve when they were to meet with the tribal chieftain and then prepare him for the coming of the ships of sail, the Heemskerck and the Zeehaen.

Night's morning darkened enough that the vampires roused from their ineffable lethargy and went straight to the chieftain of the Te Maori, as they called themselves, and conversed at length. Ahuriri's council members sat with him as they listened to these creatures that had dropped from the sky.

Yes, he had been informed of their coming by one of his female gatherers. The awe with which she described the twosome and their transformation impressed Ahuriri. It even frightened him to a degree; though he was loath to admit that to anyone. But that these beings had been winged and then in an instant had been of fully human shape made him think of gods on earth. Yet he was fearless and planned on standing toe to toe with them.

For now, he and his cohorts simply listened to what they had to say.

Mikilenia began thus, "In the turn of several moons, you will need to prepare for the approach of two canoes like you have never encountered. They use sails as you use sails. But the size of these vessels is huge; larger than any watercraft that you have ever observed.

"These ships have monstrous devices attached to their deck that can throw gigantic fireballs into your midst and kill all who have the misfortune of appearing in their path. You must beware of more than just this. These sailors will have smaller metallic objects called guns that throw tiny and fast moving fireballs at you. Those fireballs cannot crush you but will penetrate your flesh and make you bleed to death."

Ahuriri did not believe what his ears told him he was hearing. "We have spears and clubs at our disposal at all times. We fear nothing. We dance, we sing thundering war chants and we have strength to spare within all of us. You must be wrong!"

Though Anteekwa was female and therefore diminished in the male Te Maori eyes, she was of a breed that set her apart. So they listened intently when she pounded them with her words. "Mikilenia is righteous in what he tells you. Your muscled torsos will simply crumple when a bullet passes through you. Your dances and your tribal chants will avail you not at all. The huge cannon will mangle you to death on the spot. And your enemy will not even have to get close to you to do this. So your spears and clubs will be useless as well."

Breathlessly, Mikilenia took over where Anteekwa left off. "These men, and they will all be males ready to fight, are completely different from you. You are dark and massive. They have white and pale skin mostly that hangs on a leaner frame than yours.

"They will shock you in their difference. You may pause before engaging them because of this. And even then you might make the mistake of thinking that they are weak because they are not burly. Their weapons are superior to yours. And it is their weapons, not their physique, which will cause your downfall if you do not heed our truths here!"

A council member said with a doubt tinged statement, "Were we to trust your words, what is our proper plan for attack then?"

Anteekwa bent into the crowd of circled faces. "You were there a moon ago. You were with us as we shared our energies. Mikilenia and I have allied ourselves with you. We have demonstrated that forcefully. There is the foundation of your trust in our guidance."

"Do you credit our words as worthy? Yes or no!" shouted Mikilenia. This exclamation captivated and convinced Ahuriri. He revered potency and this man was potent. Last evening persuaded the villagers to lean the undead direction but this discourse cemented the bond forever after.

"They are worthy. So what must we do?"

"I will reveal that to you immediately. And it is easy. Scare them but do so wisely.

"Exhort your warriors into the traditional frenzy. Go to your canoes after. But keep those lusting for blood distant from the newly landed ships. Watch the reactions of your foe faithfully.

"It is most likely that they will want to observe you rather than engage you. Discourage their landing even though they are not a war party. Possibly they will leave you alone and never set foot on your shores. They may stay on ship as they document what they notice. They will truly not want harm to befall anyone at all.

"She and I will go ourselves and confront the leader of these ships. It is our duty to protect you as we also chose to serve ourselves.

"She and I have a score to settle with them. It may take a span of time but settle it we will!"

There was little left to be declared in this ultimately not kept promise but Ahuriri was curious of what sounded like outlandish beings to him. "Where do these ships come from?"

Anteekwa answered this question. "Your ancestor's origins, you have told us, were from islands south of here. These men traveled long distances from the north of you. Their direction is exactly the opposite of that of your ancestors."

"Do they dress differently than we do?"

"Their lands are cold and harsh. So yes, they wear much more clothing than you." Mikilenia was replying in amusement now.

The Te Maori had no beginning understanding of the differences that existed between the Europeans and themselves; nor how rude their aggressiveness could be. Life was about to change radically for these natives.

Mikilenia suddenly frowned as he realized the cataclysm sailing toward these primitive peoples.

CHAPTER 13

Murderer's Bay

They had slowly meandered up the coastline and were just now considering dropping anchor as they spied a hooked portion of that shoreline which offered them the ideal site for calm waters and indefinite protection. The waters of this bay were flat and profoundly sapphire to its very bottom. Tiny globes of blazing firelight dotted the beaches and the forest's peripheral interior. Moon shine glinted off of the surface of those deceptively peaceful waters.

All vampires and many crew were alert and on deck in anticipation of an action of some kind. Visscher and Gilsemans stood alongside their Master Commander and his almost always accompanying trio. They had been fully informed of the character and style of the inhabitants that Abel felt would soon be approaching the ships. This notion of native approach was surmised as Mikilenia and Anteekwa had hindered all their seer vision, including into the minds of the rebel's allies. But it was a strong surmise as Abel had long association with Mikilenia and was astute as to the other's behavior.

The remainder of the crew that was present maintained their positions but in a relaxed fashion as they had not been told of what was likely to come. The probability was that they would not have believed their commander but they would have obeyed most assuredly. They were loosely vigilant only and watched their officers more than they watched the shore.

As was reckoned by Abel and his Janna, both the Heemskerck and the Zeehaen were approached by at least a dozen men; two or more to a boat as it varied randomly. They called out to the occupants of the European ships but the sounds were muffled. And all psychic sensorium was still being held at bay by Mikilenia and his companion so that even Abel was not capable of probing their minds to distinguish what was shouted at them.

The nearing boat, then more boats, stopped at some distance away from the tightly anchored ships. Abel noticed the unique structure of the native's boats. These boats consisted of two long canoes lashed together, with planks laid for seating. One of these now seven gathered boats had a very high prow to it and certainly carried the leader upon it.

Abel ascertained that it was now reasonable to send his quartermaster and six oarsmen by the Heemskerck's small boat to the Zeehaen. He wanted to warn Holleman to be on his guard but not overly so as it seemed that no hostile boarding party was imminent.

It was as they returned that the tiny craft was set upon and rammed viciously by one of the canoes. Abel had not seen or expected this and it elicited his wrath immediately. He heard the swats of wood contacting bone and the futile cries of his comrades. He realized instantly that four of his own had been fatally wounded. But he was unable to go to them without revealing his demon identity. So he had to stand paralyzed as did Janna, Catrione and Eumann.

By God he seethed, he would right this wrong and find a method to make these heathen suffer. There had been no provocation and the cruelty of the attack went to his core. That thought propelled him forward.

He and Eumann simultaneously raced to the Heemskerck's sloop, piled in and were lowered to the water's surface. From there, they oared as if purely single-minded and crazed. The speed that they generated was blinding and their oars blistered what tiny waves existed. They reached the three remaining thrashing bodies and they pulled the quartermaster and two others over the side of the sloop in fluid motion that only the undead possessed.

The quartermaster gasped out, "It was just one canoe. The rest retreated and looked in shock. But they could not restrain the one and it hit us broadside in a blur."

"You are alive and they will pay somehow soon enough, quartermaster!"

The sloop returned as quickly as it had left and was raised up to the yachts deck and all spilled from it. Abel and Eumann, as well as the nearby crew, assisted the survivors.

Abel shouted for cannons to be blasted instantly. Many loads were shot into the air. None managed a direct hit though as all the canoes had scurried out of reach of the armament of the Europeans.

Abel ordered them to stop firing. And they did.

The curling smoke from the cannon's fusillade simply reminded Abel of the futility of avenging the deaths of his four men in this manner.

Abel turned to his crew and screamed, "We will not leave here until we have dealt with these savages as they deserve! And they deserve no mercy!

"This is to be called Murderer's Bay from this moment on!"

Abel went to the rail and slammed his fists on it over and over. Then he bent to that rail and heaved breath after breath.

Eumann went to Abel immediately then. Janna and Catrione froze in place as they were afraid that they might expose their disguise and act somehow feminine and compassionate in their desperation to pacify and calm their revered leader. So they hung back and left Eumann to find succor for Abel.

Eumann put his hands on Abel's shoulders and braced him strongly. He whispered into Abel's ear, "You cannot show yourself this way in front of the crew! It is not befitting you or your position. Straighten and stand tall with me now!"

Abel had enough sense to reply to Eumann, "Eugenias, absolutely, absolutely I will!"

And the two stood together. Abel hushed his rasping inhalations and peered without hesitancy at the men surrounding him. His aura of authority came to him in full force suddenly; the entity had recovered and he and Abel were powerful and in control again.

Speaking slowly, calmly and with a dignity that was not to be questioned, Abel pronounced to all, "We will not run. Ever. This was a horrible deed done to us that requires a return response. And we shall give them that response so that what happened here tonight will never be forgotten or repeated.

"That's a promise that I know that we can all agree upon."

All raised their voices and the echo of "Aye!" ricocheted off the walls of the ship and then out into the bay.

Night was coming to a close and Abel, Janna, Eumann and Catrione were cloistered back in their shelter. Caskets were opened and ready to receive them.

But Abel had a bit more that he had to utter. "Is this violence engraved upon this new land? Is there no alternative to intimidation, warfare and death?

"Somehow, some of the meaning of our existence, existence as beings only in life's shadow, has to be intertwined with human quality of life. Purpose provides meaning. And I ask you, what is our purpose?"

Catrione intoned, "I find it difficult to answer that question. There is a paradox which confounds me. And that paradox is that as I hunger to help the creatures that we once were, I also cannot continue my own survival without feeding on their blood. What of that? How do I balance that? Tell me Abel. Can you?"

A hush came upon them, the bright of day was at the brink and they had no choice but to enclose themselves and sleep the dark sleep.

Events were set to boil and even the promise of avenging the four dead was forgotten in the midst of the oncoming swirl.

CHAPTER 14

Nunuku Enobled

Nunuku vibrated through the chords of his mind. Nunuku had stolen all of his dreams while he slept through the dawn, noontime and of the afternoon too. Nunuku was the answer to his question that he had posed those twelve hours ago. This name blasted his senses and the entity unequivocally understood that his master had planted this name in his skull.

The name encompassed Abel's ever widening path to purpose and meaning and also to plant the seed of an alternative to the Te Maori's perpetually warring condition.

Abel replied to the others that they must follow him without hesitation and fly the dark and motionless summer hot sky too. They had to be quick and surreptitious about it as one bat in flight was a hardly noticeable receding dot while four were not. Abel instructed them, "Each launch yourself one at a time in thirty second spans. That is all that we can do to be invisible."

He surged with energy and exploded out of their chamber, then the master commander's quarters and into horizon's expanses. Janna followed thirty seconds on his heels and blew into the star flecked heavens behind her

Abel. Catrione was next and Eumann the last as he always was in thought to protect their flank on any journey.

Instinctively, the entity swooped along atmospheric currents and began to pass over an archipelago of islands that stretched at great length. Signals were to be given to him one after another as he neared the individual who bore the name Nunuku proudly and resolutely. Challenges throbbed in this man's domain and the entity was aware of his ability to change an entire culture's behavior. Crosscurrents of time and events had coalesced perfectly for this to provide a scope of opportunity beyond the imagining.

They all took in the beauty of the largest of these islands as they descended at the same sharp angle that Abel did. Off shore of this sometimes verdant and hilly island was a shadow of rock that was submerged but sloped gradually upward to merge with all that was above the sea. Janna's presumption in flight was that the exposed land sat atop a rise that reached to the sea floor. How magnificent, she wondered, was the fullness of that mountain were it entirely visible?

The margins of the island blended and flowed one into the other as sheer cliffs, then swells of sand dunes, flat and pristine strands of gleaming bleached beaches with gemlike lagoons and lakes interspersed. Streams were scarce and mountains were nonexistent. At most, Janna bestowed the name of mounds on these scant projections. And she was well versed and familiar with these shapes as, in her incarnation as Minkitooni, she had lived in the multi-mounded city of Cahokia.

The wind had a way of pounding upon them but it at least was not a frigid blast of air that they encountered as it was these islands brief summer. They were currents that surprised in their sudden warmth as the quick burst of a kiln's unexpected open door might surprise one standing nearby. The four were not familiar with strong puffs of hot air. Yet as they quickly acclimatized, its regular reoccurrence upon their faces satisfied them.

The lagging two were impressed by the thick forests and occasional large trees whose branches dangled almost horizontally in the lee of the wind. Neither was impressed by the swamps and bogs and spare heath that scantily dressed the surface of much of the ground.

Abel found himself drawn to smoke rising from a plateau's escarpment edge and followed the burnt odor to its source. They struck the hard surface of the earth and at the same time they morphed from bat to human form. The four found themselves standing between two swarthy men, one wielding a short knife and the other not moving at all and weaponless.

In the blink of an eye, they observed the shallow gashes on the belly of the motionless individual. Instinctively, just before the vampires spun around, Abel barely uttered, "You are Nunuku." The whirl of motion was so rapid and forceful that the energy generated knocked the knife from the hand of the attacker. As that knife spun away from the collective group, the frightened native bowed to the unknown creatures and never even thought of lunging for his knife.

Abel walked to the two stones cradling the knife and he picked it up. He drew up to the bleeding Nunuku. He proffered the knife to him and Nunuku took it calmly and without hesitation. It was as if this was exactly what was meant to be and the chieftain did not question any of what was happening before him.

In a symbolic gesture, he wiped the blood from the blade and then threw the weapon over the edge of the sloping cliff. Everyone heard the clang as the blade bounced down the stony escarpment and then the thunk of the wooden shaft as it cartwheeled off the rough surface too.

Abel turned once again and spoke to the submissive native. "You will soon understand the necessity for saving the life of your adversary. And he will no longer be your adversary ever again. He is astute and you nearly took that away from your people; a people who must follow his pronouncement."

Again, he turned. "Nunuku, you stood your ground. You were not absolutely certain that you were correct in your beliefs. But you stood by them and were willing to die for them. You were not willing to lift a weapon even as you were scarred and very likely to lose your life in the process. Your old enemy, now your ally, would have ripped your belly apart, watched you die and then fed on your flesh too.

"I am here to tell you that you may trust me implicitly and that you are a right thinking leader. Your survival is testimony to the fact that you have a hallowed message to take to your tribe; all of the many warring tribes on this island as a matter of fact. And that word of yours is the word of peace. You will utter it and insist that all warring accoutrements and behaviors will cease and desist as of this moment. No one on this island will ever take the blood of another nor will they ever eat human flesh again.

"I am here to convince you that those acts of warfare and cannibalism are now forbidden. Your mana will grow vastly because of this change in attitude.

"Once you have expressed to your followers that new ways are upon them, your pronouncement will go down forever in history as Nunuku's Law. It must be unalterable for you, the people of this island and all of their generations to ensue.

"This is great and you are a man ennobled. The exceptional attitude of those on this island will be remembered and cherished long after your flesh has met with the one God that I know to be true and infinite.

"Go now. Make it be known.

"Then we will celebrate by the fire that has been burning and has guided us to your location."

As if without thought, Nunuku went forward and led his tribes into a manner that was rarely revered but should have always been.

Abel's purpose had been laid out to him upon his awakening. And it was an awakening that, though he rebelled occasionally, was truly his destiny.

His master was wise beyond time and space.

CHAPTER 15

Shifting Passion

Her thoughts were not available to him but he had a keen awareness of her presence within the nearby environs. And he was grossly tortured by this closeness of hers to him. He even went so far as to believe that he was able to smell her natural scent wafting in waves; and in waves, he was overcome, then undone. It was then that the drawn curtains of his mind fluttered in the breeze of his anguish and his passions and desires leaked out.

And it was then, when he was least composed and minimally vigilant that Anteekwa finally understood Mikilenia's true heart. He had never loved her as she loved him. His love was reserved for Janna and Anteekwa was suddenly awash with a bile and anger that enveloped and absorbed her essence.

She had been in the midst of her routine hunt for blood to quell her vampire's appetite when Mikilenia's uncontrolled emotions whooshed her way. It was like a gust, a brief blown wind, and then a vanishing; after which, all was in disarray. And her deepest feelings were now in tumult and the shock for her was pounding at each and every one of her sensibilities!

She resisted screaming. But she so wanted to scream at him, "How could you use me as you did!? I killed for you! I stripped and writhed openly with you and for you and I stayed by your side always! And you, you bastard, kept me as forever second in your heart! You are vile and beyond redemption, Mikilenia. And oh how I hate you now!"

She had to chase her needs for sustenance first but then planned on dealing with the one she had anticipated spending an eternity with. This eternity of the heart had turned out to be such a flickering candle where the sputtering glow darkened and then was gone. Even eternity was a deceptive illusion for immortals, she thought, as she pounded through the terrain in search of prey.

The long wooden spear darted past her and she realized the danger of her raging and ragged attention. If that spear had been inches closer, she would have been staked through the heart and eternity's brevity would have been fully upon her. Her heart and her being, she understood, would have burst into a brief explosion of light, searing heat and then a rain of her ashes upon the ground below; her existence shuttered forever. That could have been her true eternity.

But this spear had missed her and she meant to find the one who threw it.

And she knew her exaggeration in her emotional maelstrom. The spear would have had to have been of a certain wood or of a silver tip, otherwise she would have come to no harm.

In a blur of speed, she winged to the ground and instantly transformed into her human form.

She spied him before he spied her. She reached into his mind and perceived that he had been returning to a small Te Maori warrior's encampment that was located far deeper in the forest. He had miles to go and had not eaten for many hours. He was famished and that was why he had attempted to make her his meal. Now, it seemed, he was to become her meal.

She bounded in front of him and blocked his path. He was stunned as well to find a dark female beauty out in the woods alone at this late hour. He briefly wondered her sanity and her strength.

She gave him no opportunity to come to any conclusions. She was upon his throat in a rush. He was a massive male specimen and he had more than ample blood for her present needs. The fear flashing from his eyes goaded her even more. This was to be a sumptuous feast. And beyond that, she fed hugely on his disbelief that he was about to die at the hands of a female. In his last moments, he comprehended that this female was hell sent and he gave her his neck in submission and capitulation. He had no ability or desire to resist her. His life was hers to take. They both were aware of that simultaneously.

That cessation of resistance intrigued her. She did not lap at his carotid yet. Even more strongly than her belly's needs, that intrigue went deeply and directly to her loins. This was no usual man. He recognized the order of the universe and that she was superior. He was of that kind of intelligence and dignity. She had to explore this further.

And with all that had slapped at her in regards to Mikilenia, she was in need of flexing her power sexually. She wanted to have this man. And she would have this man.

She took his face in her hands and gently susurrated, "Lie still on the grass here. Ignore its wet and rough surface. If anything but your cock moves, you are dead. Pant, moan but move nothing otherwise."

He said only, "I will."

"From this second on, you say no words unless it is to beg me for your release. Do you understand that?"

He only nodded his head in the affirmative.

"Reach your hands above your head and clasp one hand upon the other. Hold them there. Spread your legs wide for me. Close your eyes and do not reopen them!"

He did exactly that.

She simply ripped his flaxen coverings top and bottom down the center and gently laid them to both of his sides. He was exposed but had something dry to lie upon. It also smoothed the rough and cold surface beneath him.

He was massive and well-muscled as she had expected from a soldier of these people. Behind his facial tattoos, he was handsome as well. But even in its flaccid state, she saw the prowess of his organ. Its coloring fascinated her also. When she drew his foreskin back, the large head of his cock was in very light contrast to his very dark shaft. And this was not the coloration that she expected. Oh my, she inhaled; it was neither black nor pink. Instead, it was albino pale and it mesmerized her as she gently bent to kiss and coax this already large staff of his to life.

This joining was bound to be anything but ordinary.

She held his round, soft flesh in both of her hands. And then she very slowly stroked his length and on the down stroke licked at his tender flesh there. She tongued his tiny opening. She then froze her strokes and squeezed his hardening column tightly. His circumference pushed against her pressure and she found her hands slowly opened up by his expanding size. The constriction of her hands around his manhood trapped his blood in his cockhead and it appeared as if it were hotly glowing.

His growing size was dramatic but the contrast of colors, head then shaft, were vivid and goaded her excitement more and more. In spite of his fear, that very fear was being caressed away expertly and quickly. His cock magnetized her and she placed all of his cockhead in her mouth now and sucked on him with a heavy pull. She watched him while he erected and made sure that he did not move. His arms remained clasped, legs remained widespread and his eyes were still shut tightly.

He was trembling and his breathing was labored. She wanted exactly that.

As he continued to expand under her touch, Anteekwa felt the definite throb of his one large vein. The throb pounded her palm and she felt the pulse of her clitoris moving in perfect rhythm with his.

He moaned softly when she released him from her mouth and hands. She had to remove her own clothing now. Her nipples and reddened teardrop above her opening were too demanding for her to ignore them further.

She was the one panting as she held her breasts to his lips to taste. "You may suck on my nipples. Twist and press them between your fingers hard. Pull on the talisman and make me burn for you. I want you to be able to see how big and long they can become for you."

He did that and then she commanded, "Put your hands back above your head now!"

His breaths, after touching her very full and pendulous breasts tipped with her thick black nipples, were rasping in his throat.

She brought her hips up to his mouth, spread her slick coated nether lips and pushed them upon his lips. He waited for her direction though his cock jerked and dripped clear dew in his absolute craving for her.

"Do it to me! Lick me. Suck it! Yes, now!"

He did not hesitate then and drew her red bead into his mouth and lashed his tongue over it back and forth, up and down. Anteekwa's juices gushed into his mouth at this and she moaned ravenously. Her tiny ass quaked as she was ministered too and she threw her head back. Her raven hair cascaded down to tickle his abdomen.

She was fraught and had to have him. She broke from his suction and stood, stepped rearward and squatted over his now huge tube. She guided his pale cockhead into her wet cleft and sank down upon his pole. She took it all and was surprised at that. It filled her exquisitely and she continued to vibrate throughout her body.

She did not move for a moment and took his hands from above his head and placed them on her breasts. He pulled on her talisman and she shuddered in ecstasy. She placed her palms flat on his chest and pinched them repeatedly. His cock became even more swollen inside of her as she did this and she began to rise and fall slowly over his livid cock. She was glove to his fist.

She rode him faster and faster. He lifted his hips to her so that she felt it all so deeply.

Her cunt climaxed around his shaft in a shaking surge of release. The massage of her vaginal tunnel upon him then savaged his restraint and his torso spasmed upward as his come shot against her interior intensely. It was a long length before he was able to quell his cock.

She laid the side of her head on him and listened to the beat of his heart. He slowly dropped back down to the ground.

"You are saved. And you are mine."

A shift of passion had abruptly occurred for her.

CHAPTER 16

Creation Story

They were pleased to be with him and he was pleased to be with them.

Nunuku was satisfied with his proclamation and the impending peaceful results of that proclamation. Even his nemesis had gone with him and had praised the notion of tranquility alongside Nunuku. The twosome had inspired the tribes as the new word was uttered and it took no convincing for the Te Moriori natives to adopt the fresh approach.

So now, nights later, they sat in a large circle and Nunuku initiated the telling of the early rendering of his people with a muted but especially pleased intonation. "In the beginning, darkness was everywhere. Heaven and earth both dwelt in this darkness and had forever.

"Earth provided succor for the heavens and the heavens provided succor for the earth. They clung to one another as only two frightened children can do. Much time passed and they stayed close to each other.

"The spirit of Rangitokona became frustrated with the fears of heaven and earth. He rose up finally and asked them to separate. As expected, they would not and hugged each other even more tightly at the suggestion. So Rangitokona used all of his mighty strength and pushed them apart with great force. He immediately propped the heavens up with ten pillars, one atop the other. This took the place of the earth's prior support of the heavens.

"And Rangitokona chanted this as he worked, 'Rangitokona prop up the heaven, Rangitokona prop up the morning. The pillar stands in the baldness of heaven, in the bare part of heaven. The pillar stands, the pillar of heaven.'

"Suddenly there was a flash and for the first time ever, light appeared. And the world and skies became visible and alive.

"Earth from the earth was piled high by Rangitokona and the first man was created. He was called Tu. Rangitokona's incantation as he did this went, 'Heap it in the waving of the tree, heap it in the pattern of the tree, heap it in the finishing of the tree, heap it, it grows; heap it, it lives, the heaven lives. Aieeeee! All are heaped up, and they live and may pray to heaven which stands on pillars above.'

"Tu was great and his descendants multiplied vigorously.

"Some say that Tu was Te Maori first and then that he was Te Moriori second. That is blasphemy. They are wicked and we are not. We have never been them and they have never been us.

"This first group, sired by Tu and called 'heaven born', endured thirty prosperous generations. Next came twenty six generations of equally prosperous peoples.

"Finally, Te Aomarama was born and his name meant 'the world of light'. His son was magnificent and he was Rongomaiwhenua.

"His name meant 'song of the land'. He had a brother as well. He was as massive as an ocean god. So he was named Rongomaitere. It was this brother who braved the vast ocean waves with his people and was the first to travel here. He also left directions for a return to their original homeland in case later peoples were wistful and chose to leave.

"This is how the race of the Hamata came to be. They sprang from the earth and on the earth they remain.

"From then until now, two migrations of visitors arrived onto this land.

"The first occurred when two tribes in land miles from our beloved Rekohu, fertile soil that we sit on this dark but auspicious night, fought and it ended in the death of one righteous individual. It began as a lover's quarrel and finished with the blood of one covering the ground.

"The wrath of the dead partner's tribe forced a quick departure of those who were allied to the one who had taken his partner's life. Several canoes fled to the waters and rowed rapidly away. After long and difficult travels, only one canoe arrived safely here.

"These survivors grew the Hamata population. Yet Rekohu had land aplenty and all were satisfied.

"The second of the two migrations came a generation on. The son of the chieftain who had expelled the first tribe became curious and desired to go in search of the lost tribe. He was Moe and he took his family and an experienced crew of men and left all that was familiar. He had no notion as to his direction but certain bright stars, ocean currents, bird's paths and wind patterns brought him to our island over time.

'They were sick and starving upon their arrival but were nourished by us and were brought back to a vigorous health.

"The Hamata, the Wheteina of the first influx and the Rauru of the second influx all lived in relative harmony together for a span of time.

"Sadly, clashes, then battles broke out in pockets over the island. It even spread to other islands in our beautiful chain of islands.

"Then a very rash deed was executed and Moe and his followers were burned alive in their sleeping huts in a single night.

"And that is why I was as you found me. I was on the verge of denouncing violence and commanding peace. But I was uncertain of my power and strength of belief, even as present chieftain, and was unable to call out the word peace. And then there was my rival, who did not want peace and was willing to see my entrails spread in the dirt in order to preserve conflict.

"Yet he sits next to me now!"

The men embraced and the glad hush after was deep and tranquil.

"Then you of Rangi, our heaven, intervened.

"Your blessings upon our island have proven rich and fortuitous!

"I will always be aware of the principles of peace and cooperation forever more.

"And ultimately, I must thank the four of you for the absolute clarity of mind that you have given me. For my life as well as I would not be alive was it not for you. No matter my quiet uncertainties then, the one thing that I knew absolutely was that I was not going to use any weapon or force against anyone."

The creation story of the Te Moriori touched the undead. And it was evident that the undead were not immune from gentler feelings. Truly though, it was only the entity inside of Able who still had to be convinced of that. Janna was already the darling of what was good. Catrione constantly atoned for her acts with her son. And Eumann had a teacher's nature from the very beginning. His intelligence manifested itself in wanting to support others who might not have been so bestowed.

The entity was so tamed in comparison to his beginnings. Yet he, of them all, these four, had the most disquiet about it; almost as if he grieved his vanishing monster of machination and ferocity. Yet his impulses as he aged drew him to a softening of both thought and behavior. Should he be ashamed of this? He imagined not.

And why not? It wasn't so much an intellectual exercise for him. It was that, as he observed his new cloak of behavior, he felt decent. It was simple and went beyond words or explanation.

This sense compelled him to look at Nanuku.

And subtly smile.

CHAPTER 17

Growing Fascination

As the tiny smile disappeared, Abel asked, "What are the traditions that your culture holds dear?"

Nunuku understood that Abel, the other three also, felt an identification of some sort with his people. That was what stoked the growing fascination that Abel had for Nunuku's island community. Being aware of that, Nunuku's chest expanded with pride.

"I say this so that you four know that my Law is not without some aggression. Men will take offense and get angry. And the urge to strike out then becomes uncontrollable. But that harm will be minimized as there are rules that must be observed. The only weapon allowed is a long thin stick. The only method allowed is to thrash each other with those sticks and as soon as bleeding occurs, the fighting must stop abruptly. The one bleeding loses the issue at stake.

"Otherwise, our culture has tended to be a gracious one. And, now that the recent rift has been settled, there will be no more outbreaks of violence ever again."

Janna leaned in and was sweetly curious. "How do you survive what has to be a harsh and long cold season?"

"The islands can be so cold and inhospitable throughout all of the seasons except this one. We farm very little food as almost nothing grows well here. Our sustenance comes principally from the arms of the sea or the vast chambers of the sky. From the blue waters, we eat fish and seal. In vast regard for the seal, we never leave their carcasses to rot out in the open. Those carcasses, their fur, are always used as clothing for warmth. From the skies above, we find birds in abundance. The bird that is preferred has black plumage and a white breast. We call it Taiko and it is delicious. The albatross is very plump and tasty and we often substitute it for the Taiko.

"There is a tale of the wild growing fern root that we devour relentlessly." Nunuku guffawed at this. He knew that it was a not very appealing staple that was critical to their health and nurture. Children most especially hated the detestable weed but they all ate it nonetheless.

"The root originated in this fashion. When the earth and sky were separated, two of three brothers fought. The one brother, who had split mother earth from father heaven, was attacked by his brother who felt that their parents had been disrespected. The third brother, the god of uncultivated foods, fled into the folds of their mother in fright. The fronds of our saving plant are said to be Haumia's hair sticking up out of mother earth.

"Its importance to us is supreme. And to make it more palatable, here is how we prepare these fronds to eat. They are tall and are best harvested as spring approaches summer. They are dried and then soaked in water. They are roasted, boiled or steamed. But that is not the end of it. The women pound away at them and that divides the edible flesh from the green fibers. The paste from this process is formed into cakes and sweetened, then eaten. Even then it is grudgingly swallowed."

"Are there foods that you do like?" Catrione was now very curious. They all remembered what it had been like to salivate over morsels of prime meats and delicious desserts.

"Two other foods, the kumara and the karaka berry are very satisfying. The kumara is sweet, orange and when prepared correctly, so soft and delicious. The karaka berry is useful too. But it can be very dangerous. It must be prepared exactingly or it may cause a thrashing of limbs and frothing of the mouth that kills you. Before it can flavor our bread, it must be baked, trampled and then soaked in a stream for days to leach out the poison. We dry and store the berry kernels then. The breads that they grace are given only to the select few."

Eumann guffawed. "That is much effort for a kernel that does so little for the bread and is reserved for the revered few; and can kill you."

Abel turned Eumann's way and gave him a stern look that silenced Eumann immediately.

"Speaking of our leaders, we chose them not from their lineage but from their abilities. I am skilled in catching albatross and in the methods of diplomacy. I imagine it is more the skills of diplomacy that led me to my present position." He grinned after saying this.

Janna was in wonderment at the quiet oratorical skills that Nunuku possessed. He was capable of telling his people's various sagas, their traditions and the poetry of their lives in a blend that was persuasive and magnetic to her.

"You do not ornament your skin as we observed on men who attacked our ships when we first arrived."

Nunuku replied softly to Janna, "Those men who attacked you are a disgrace. They are not of this island. And that is the simple method to know who we are and who they are. We do not wear tattoos of any kind. And they are clothed in tattoos. We do not wear rings in our ears either. And, of course, they practice that habit.

"Body ornamentation is not emphasized here.

"But we do practice the arts in a much more unique manner.

"Let me show you one of our tools for carving through the bark of the tree."

Nunuku went to a corner of the thatched hut that they huddled in and returned with an instrument that was entirely stone; the handle was stone and so was the sharper head. It appeared more a brute weapon than anything to be used for artistic carvings. Each vampire handled it carefully before passing it back to the chieftain.

"Rise with me and I will show you one of our cherished trees."

All, including Nunuku's advisors, followed him to a very large karaka tree that had beautifully executed drawings sliced and cut from the supple tree covering. Abel wondered at how such a clumsy device, as was their adze, could be singly used to bring these wood figures to a vivid reality.

"These pictures mark significant events for us; or the burial of an important Moriori. They signify what we hold close and that allow us to survive. A fish of great size, an extraordinary catch, is engraved on a trees outer layer. The same is true after a successful capture of many albatross. I have managed that over and over.

"But I am one to rarely brag. So I will stop now."

"One more question please, Nunuku."

The chieftain inclined his head toward the gorgeous Janna whose eyes seemed most especially ignited by this talk. Were he younger, he would gather her to his heart.

Janna queried this, "Again, there were differences between your people and the men who killed four of our crew. They had small boats that seemed to move so quickly. They were built so that there was a canoe attached to another canoe with a platform between them. Do you have anything like that?"

Nunuku lifted one eyebrow as he answered her. "It is so that they have craft like you describe. No, we do not have that."

He sat very upright suddenly and puffed up his chest for the second time that eve. "We have something that rides the waters even better than anything possessed by the Te Maori. We construct our waka so ably that it cannot be copied. The boat is buoyed by a weave of flax on the outside bottom and long strands of kelp on the inside bottom. Sea water flows through the tiny crisscrossed openings that the flax provides. This bottom is topped off by the remainder of our vessel. This special bottom means that our creations never tip over or sink.

"The waka is our delight."

With that, the vampires departed in camaraderie. Once they transformed and took flight, the leader of the Te Moriori and his advisors did not fear them.

Instead, they raised their voices in song that filled the air with joy.

And that joy helped propel the bats forward.

CHAPTER 18

Endless Reverberations

Catrione had first collided into and then fed upon the blood of an albatross as the four had swooped home. Because of this, the other three were still probing the surroundings for their own sustenance. So, Catrione sat alone in the confines of the master commander's quarters. In their caution, she was dressed as Claudios too.

Her fatigue regarding the endless reverberations of what she and her son had foolishly managed to do those eight hundred years ago was heavy. Those reverberations seized and spat upon her happiness often and powerfully. She had been attempting to atone for those actions since the tragic occurrence. And it was the impact upon her son's life that most concerned her. She felt that her strength of rectitude since then bound her to acting sensibly. Mikilenia had let their joining peck at his heart until the rhythms of that heart found no rhythm whatsoever; so anger was Mikilenia's constant companion.

She hoped that her revelation to Mikilenia earlier, obvious though it was, might mean a sane coming of behavior for him. She was saddened for Anteekwa but that one was of definite secondary concern.

Catrione reviewed the circumstances for just one more of an infinite set of times.

The confluence of events then had surged over them all and the dark seed of unfamiliar circumstances set bizarre behaviors rocking forward.

She was a young woman who had had a son. She was equally a princess of a great nation that was ultimately absorbed by an even greater nation. She had been Pictish and had been captive of the greater Gaelic nation. The Gael who claimed her totally was a thug who did not care for her being but only her ravishing looks. Her brilliance only intimidated him and he treated her ruthlessly and without regard. This was Mikilenia's father.

Some of his father's impulsive and incautious traits had been passed to his son.

Yet she loved this son of hers in spite of his ambivalence towards her. He was her flesh and blood and her only child. And who was to argue with that?

In discontent and sadness, Catrione sought out other lovers. And she found that perfect person in the guise of her son's teacher, Eumann. She was unable to resist him and his tender and truly loving approach to her. They remained a pair together these eight hundred years later. And with her pleasure in finding her mate, it tormented her to have to see her son's unhappiness unfurl through the centuries.

Now to attempt to bring her reflections back to what was pivotal for those impacted.

She had learned of the existence of the entity in these years as her partner had been inhabited by this entity and had shared his soul with the demon. Shared hardly explains the extent of the entity's control over Eumann. And the entity had been so clever in disguising himself. She had no idea of his demon infusion until Eumann himself revealed his condition to her. She had been overwhelmed simply by this knowledge but had been further buffeted by the fact that it was impermanent for Eumann. The entity had spoken directly to her then and fed her the fact that his abilities were unique amongst the undead. He left his skins at the behest of a nebulous master.

She was dealing with the impact of that possibility in addition.

Then war had broken out again. And her son was of advanced enough age that he was expected to engage the enemy. To add to that, not only was her son to accompany her husband in this battle supreme but her husband demanded that her partner be involved as well. And even though Eumann had already transformed her into a vampire, her heart still fluttered in anxiety.

And her flutter was so justified. The battle brought unforeseen results; their surprise attack was trampled by the enemy and her husband was slain gruesomely. His death might have brought joy if that was the singular effect of the clashing of armies. The entity, to save the life of her son, had been commanded to leave her lover's skin and pierce the skin of her son so that the entity stood Mikilenia up against his attackers and brought life to the young warrior and victory to his troops. Mikilenia went by the name Cinaed as this happened.

But Eumann suffered being human once more.

She was disconcerted by this perfect storm of incidents and was reeling at so many abrupt changes. Her son was now joined with the entity and her love was weak and disempowered.

The final triggers to all this was the massive celebration of war's success, too much available mead, and the tension that she and her son experienced in their proximity to each other on that fateful evening. That tension had reached a height for her that, mixed with the mead, became an impulse and energy that was like a writhing snake twisting out of her grasp. And so she was bitten. And she took that opportunity to swing and sway before her son in an erotic display that brooked only come hither paradise for him. He was awash in as much mead as she was. And she was ungodly beautiful then as she was now. She used that to melt his resistance. As the melt occurred, he yielded to the heat and throb of his cock.

Her nipples were huge in excitement then, and she, in diaphanous top, laid them at his eager lips. He sucked her dark, thick tips through the material when he was able to catch them in the arch of their sway. The glint, the passion, in their eyes had blotted out any clarity that had been there.

Oh god, she had led him then to a chamber where they were alone and private and that was their ultimate undoing. A web of poisonous desire had broken through their inhibitions and they both succumbed to it. Even now, this reflection of the past caused her fount to lubricate and flow. She hated that the intimacies between them, and they partook of every intimacy conceivable, was engraved upon her psyche and sexual organs forever.

How much further was she going to recollect upon this frightful and life altering escapade between them. It crushed her that she, as the parent most particularly, vampire or no, had not only not stemmed the tide but had gladly been the tide's beginning. She wanted to scratch at her loins and scrape away the madness of that night.

She could not. In eight hundred years, she had not found the magic to soothe herself and brush away the taint.

Yet, back then, she had managed to find a means to opening her mouth and confessing all to Eumann. He had pressed for her honesty at the time and she had poured forth the tortuous bile of that honesty. He had loved her for her courage though in revealing the details to him. He felt that she was brave and magnificent. And soon thereafter, being vampire, she transformed this exceptional man back to that of the undead so that she could wander this shadow life with him for eternity.

The problem that arose for her son, that came from mother and sons' sexual effrontery, was that he had lost and then found his true love again. The incest incident had been sandwiched between his loss and the years later when he found his Aiobheean again. And lo, that Aiobheean, was now the lovely Janna who draped herself upon Abel's arm.

She was twice lost to him. How could that be? Well, her son had never exposed their atrocity to his lustrous queen. He had buried the necessity of telling her. It was a tragic mistake. Aiobheean then discovered the fact, was utterly shocked and left him. And she had remained in disgust with him to this day.

And most of it was her fault. Catrione closed her eyes and staunched the thoughts abruptly. She was overwhelmed with emotion and grief for Mikilenia.

Would repair of love lost ease her black knot of despair? Was repair forever out of reach?

CHAPTER 19

Violet Eyes

Red sustenance came to them all soon enough and then Eumann returned straight away to the master commander's quarters on the ship. Abel and Janna lofted themselves in the opposite direction. They had been imbued with good feeling since their encounter with the Te Moriori and they wanted to play those feelings out upon one another.

Crossing paths of a sudden, Janna was entranced by the large white bird that had gracefully blown right past her. She was stunned by the length of its neck and the slenderness of its long red stems for legs. Its wing span was broad and it sped by without even the remotest of effort. Janna telegraphed to Abel that they needed to follow this marvelous bird to its destination. This creature was a thing of beauty and Janna had to sate her curiosity regarding its magnificence.

It swept them far along the coastline and dove in towards a lagoon where it dipped to the water's surface and then swiftly blended in with a flock of the same birds in the margins there. This body of water gleamed in the moon's umbrella of light and its sapphire hues and clear quality was neither broken by the wind nor the wading of any bird whatsoever.

It beckoned to the both of them and they did something that was rare. They eschewed any clothing as they cut through the line of liquid so smoothly that once engulfed by it, their entry point vanished abruptly. And they saw well but the depths were so pristine that they did not need vampire strength of sight to turn their heads and blissfully smile at each other. This was the delicious romance that they had longed for earlier.

Abel felt a finger of warmth touch him. It was not Janna. But Janna felt it too as they swam side by side. They were no longer bats but instead were of human form possessing a vast ability to hold their breath and propel themselves easily forward through what felt and looked like softly resisting glass.

They followed the tiny path of the bubbles deeper into the lagoons interior. More bubbles migrated toward them in a greater rush as they cut toward what was a stony overhang that arched in the water. This formation created a tunnel-like passage that spat an onslaught of those bubbles at them. Undaunted, the duo stroked to and then through this completely water filled passage. Abel realized that they were experiencing a thermal column of water which was gushing up from the lagoon's floor and was sending now relatively superheated bubbles to the roof of the passage. This caused a dispersal of those bubbles backwards to the lagoon and forwards to some not yet found place.

They continued to follow the bubbles to the tunnel's end. It did not take long.

Suddenly, they raised their heads out of the heated sapphire pool and found themselves in a natural formation of glowing rock that was startling in its qualities. It was a domed cavern that shot a violet light to and fro. The light must have come from the minerals that formed the walls within this cavern.

Janna gasped and Abel allowed his heart beat to escalate just a bit in homage to the rock and waters combined signature.

There was the tiniest of heated mist within the chambers. Yet they saw all details as nothing obstructed vampire eyes; not even the absolute dark. And this meant that Abel easily found a carved cupped area that was large, smoothly upturned and was a ledge above the surface.

They lifted themselves onto this hammock of stone, warmed constantly by the sweeping entombed heat, and sat at its edge for a moment.

Abel took Janna's chin and held her face before him. Her luminosity was wild. Her skin was a florescent purple and, my god, as he peered into her eyes, they were a violet that burst his way. He even drew his head back for an instant as if actually struck by her violet eyes. And with the mist, the effect was even more erotic. The violet danced off her irises in a violent and irregular fashion.

He must have her now.

He placed one arm behind her back and one arm underneath her knees and, all the while kissing and whispering into her ears, then gently rotated her body and laid her carefully down.

She was so mesmerized by his desire that the stone felt like the softest feathered mattress at her back. The temperature of the cavern was as if a balm and the drops on their skin evaporated rapidly. Nature had provided them a sanctuary that christened their joining this moment as significant. The significance was yet unknown.

She cast any long term thoughts aside and sank into her flesh as it meshed with his flesh.

He leaned above her with his nearly flat palms propped upon the perfectly dry curve of granite beneath them. At first, she kept her hands against his chest so that she might gaze at his countenance that held so much beauty and value to her. She watched as the violet reflected off of his eyes also. And, though she was unaware of how ravishing the effect made her to him, she felt her yearning for him escalate incredibly.

Automatically, she leaned on her elbows and with upper arms at her side, cupped her very heavy breasts to him. She ached everywhere as he bent in and began to suck her berry stained straining nipples avidly; and it was at these sensitive thick tips of hers that she felt it utterly. And offering them to him roused the both of them further and further.

He cupped her at the moist apex of her thighs and then eased several fingers into her opening. She spread her legs wide so that the contact was made effortlessly and the feeling was made strong.

She lay back down on the stone fully and sighed as his fingers glided from her interior, over her fount and to her dark pink jewel that was rousing second by second. He touched her there over and over. Then he knelt to her Venus mound, licked the fingers that had just been inside of her and then spread her lips aside and up. Her love triangle appeared as a butterfly would and caused her tiny knob to project readily. His mouth seized on that and he drew her in deeply. His tongue caressed her there so sweetly.

Janna probed and one of her hands found the column of his that was hard and hot and so long. Its circumference was already such that she was barely able to fully grasp its shaft. And as she tried, he moaned and his cock expanded even more. So she began to stroke it fast and as firmly as she could. At one moment, she took her thumb and rubbed his dewy passion from his cock's opening all over his mushroom sized cockhead.

He adored that and trembled in lust at the sensation.

He barely paused, even between her moans and wide eyed wonderment at why he was altering such a delicious position and stroke of hand and tongue, to assist her in standing. He sat then and wanted to take the roughness of the stone, if any, and remove that possible discomfort from her. He set his legs in a spacious v shape and pumped himself to a huge size.

He rasped, "Sit on me my love. Take my cock and face away. I have to have you this way."

She did not hesitate. She clutched at his shaft, guided the reddish-purple and almost too ample cockhead into her drenched sheath. She slowly dropped her bottom over it. Once he was fully engulfed she sat on his lap and ground her loins into him. He leaned back with one arm but with the other he reached around and massaged a large breast.

She did not rise and fall upon him but simply ground into him in hip circles. Truly though, she was unable to resist and did lift up and down intermittently.

He touched and then squeezed her nipple hard. The rhythm of his fingers upon her caused her to approach that delirious point of no return. He had continued his growling in a low guttural way. It had increased frantically and he was near.

She craved this sound of his and she suddenly leapt to an orgasm that annihilated everything else. Her waves of pleasure burst from her center and those caresses upon his massive organ deep inside her dazed him.

The trigger came to him as he heard her crying and felt her body shaking with her release. He throbbed one last time and then lifted his groin up to her, both arms balancing him now, and loaded her with his love to beyond what she could save. It oozed from her around him.

She lay back into him and slowly subsided.

Their languor was brief as they sensed that daybreak was coming soon enough. It was a circadian rhythm within the undead that, regardless the circumstances, they knew. Their survival depended upon this inner clock.

Water broke upward and winged forms broke skyward.

Their Heemskerck waited.

CHAPTER 20

Finally Exposed

She was leaning over her prey as any feral dog would. She was so very pure except when she was bent by primal undead forces that gave no latitude. This was when the demon vampire was so vulnerable too. As the crimson liquid flowed from neck's gash to monster's mouth, the feeding creature had no thought or movement. As the life-juice of the large bird filled her being, she stood rooted to the ground.

Mikilenia took much delight in watching Janna. Her chin dribbled red, her eyes glazed as if in ecstasy and her strawberry blond hair hung loosely. The sucking sound excited him, yet he had already satisfied his needs. And he was going to approach her calmly. He did not desire her ire or her fright.

He took the several minutes of her feasting to settle his cock that had expanded the material of his breeches in its curled shape. He mastered his breath and his instrument slowed and then slumbered. His breeches found normal body lines at this point.

He also looked away from her heaving chest so as to show no arousal. Yet it was difficult not to gaze at her bodice, a bodice that held one of her huge breasts but did not cover the other at all. The exposed one, he had so briefly noticed, hung at considerable expanse with the aureole and nipple so pronounced. It took all of his strength to focus on her face until she was done.

Her sucking complete and the corpse dropped to the ground, Janna turned slightly as she swiped the blood from her chin. When she recognized Mikilenia there, she was torn by divergent emotions. She froze for an instant as her impulses battled each other. She was hardened by his presence but was softened by wanting to counter what he had just seen with a demonstration of her typical regard and sweetness. The latter won out. She curbed her anger and brought her reflexive smile to her face. She remained unaware of her bared breast and the cool air kept her tip tight and long.

He approached her as he comprehended that she was willing to allow him a presence with her. He had a small cloth and blotted the remaining blood from her face. Instead, though urgent in his desire to touch her protruding mound, he said, "Refill your bodice. One of your breasts beckons me and I prefer no distractions between us, even gorgeous ones."

Janna gasped and covered herself immediately.

Truly, it was to no avail, as Janna had little material making up her bodice. She rarely fed alone but it was one of those occasions where Abel was on ship tending to plans for effecting the first on land contact with the Te Maori. She had dressed casually and had not expected an audience of any kind. Mikilenia was the last face she had expected to glimpse. But here he was and in her sliver of consternation combined with her sheer surprise, she was breathing more rapidly than usual. And her chest heaved a bit right along with the labor of inhalation and exhalation.

He loved that loss of control on her part. She hated it.

"I had to find you alone Aio. I will call you that. That is who you are to me and always will be; you are my beautiful Scottish Queen who should still be at my side to this very night."

"I am Janna to you. We have no history between us as far as I am concerned. But I will, to be polite, call you by whatever name you wish to have."

"Then call me Cinaed."

"Except for that name, I will never call you that! It brings detestable images to me."

"So you are not numb to our history. That you react to my name then shows the falsity of your just uttered words. We do have a history and you know it as well as I do. And though they have passed now, we had children together; a brood that we both loved. Their images stand starkly in my memory. I visualize each and every one of their precious faces."

"You were a lying beast then, and if I had known that, I would have never been your queen or a woman bearing children for you.

"You savaged what we had when you not only laid with your mother but then never had the courage or decency to let me know that and make my own choices from that point on."

Mikilenia was fast advancing toward the point of true reckoning here. He needed her back, had missed her love for him for nigh on to eight hundred years and was determined to have his say in this finally and now.

"I had intended to tell you. And my assumption was that you would have understood and supported me considering the circumstances of those times. So much was in flux then. I was newly demon having just survived a battle that, but for the entity, I should not have survived. I was just aware of my mother as undead. My father had just been brutally beheaded. And you were lost to me, I believed; and my anguish over that very fact speared my heart repeatedly. I felt alien, confused and uncertain of anything.

"And is it not crucial that, though my mother and I did indulge our detestable desires, we understood immediately after that it was detestable and that it was never going to reoccur. I even thought about flinging my mother from the kingdom. I was disgusted with it and, as I discovered later, she was equally horrified. Does the cure not count for anything?"

Janna sighed and spoke to the core of the matter for herself, "You never told me though." These words came from her lips one at a time and each word was staccato and firm as they shot from her.

Mikilenia understood the power behind those words. He had been the perpetrator, after all. "Lazy assurance and then forgetfulness over time was a fool's blend. And that was exactly what happened with me. And I regret it. And I profusely apologize to you for that enormous oversight.

"I do have to mention one thing that almost all of us have overlooked since those many years ago; overlooked by all except the entity immediately and my mother too slowly to avoid your and my pain since our parting as Gael King and Queen."

Janna was direct with her once liege lord, "I am listening. But the wound was incredibly deep and has failed to heal at all even over eight centuries. Also, though I have hissed at you, talked the worst about you and brought my loins to another, I have loved you since then. If I had not, it never would have hurt so harshly.

"So you have my ear. But it must be significant or I will be determined to walk away from you once more."

He began. "Until my mother whispered this to me, my emotional scar that came from our separation stilled my seeing the obvious.

"The entity was inside of me when my mother and I were sexual. He had his usual powerful hand held around my spirit's throat and he was in charge. I am angry so if I seem to criticize the demon excessively, try and understand my position! He was there Aio and he could have stopped me!! Do you hear that?! He could have but . . . he . . . did . . . not!

"And he has blocked the fact from you since. And has never revealed that fact to you himself!"

Janna flinched and moaned at this revelation finally exposed. "He has always been loving toward me. He has never deviated from that!"

"It is true that he and I were both involved. He missed my mother. He had been inside Eumann awhile as he and she were lovers. He resisted no more than did I!

"Ask my mother. Better yet, ask the entity within Abel."

Janna wheeled from him and was totally intent upon confronting the entity.

CHAPTER 21

No Excuses

Minus a partner was what he was about to become. He stood stock still as her soundless shriek ricocheted against what seemed his feeble skull. The onslaught was enormous and this moment had been foreordained. He had not fought it and had no excuses for his behavior except that he had desired both females. When he had worn Eumann's mask it was appropriate, he and Catrione. When he had worn Cinaed's mask it was not appropriate, he and Catrione. It was too late to repair that damage when Janna, the once Aiobheean, was rediscovered.

And he had truly stepped over the bounds of more than civility; he had stepped over the bounds of sanctified tradition. His malevolence had stormed him then as the mead and his still roughed being let those evil impulses free. Now he was about to find ice in the coldness of the consequences hurtling towards him.

He probably could have stopped the meeting of Mikilenia and Janna had he wished it. But he was so tired of interfering in the lives of those that he truly loved. His fatigue with manipulation grabbed him long ago. So he had remained on the bow of the deck of the Heemskerck and attempted not to flinch when his incensed companion flung herself onto the wood timbers. He was shocked that she did not split them in the sheer power of her landing.

"You look at me! What have you never told me?" He allowed her to grasp his shoulders in clenched fist with long nails tearing his clothing and then gouging his very flesh in her wrath and in the torment of one scorned. She did not restrain herself and snarled at him as spittle mixed with the blood of her prior meal sprayed his face.

He bowed his head slightly and wiped dribbles away with a quick hand. She was vibrating in her need to just tear the bastard limb from limb. She and Abel knew better. She did not have the might. Had she though, she would have ripped his heart from his chest and crushed it in her bare hands.

The entity spoke sadly and quietly through Abel's mouth. "Yes, it is as was told to you. And I have no justification for what I have done.

I do love you but I had loved her too. I had sheathed my cock away and was not going to approach her in intimate caress ever again. But the demon in me was roused with her close proximity and my being flush with mead. My cock grew for her and it had its way. I did nothing to resist my yearning."

She removed her claws from him and beat on his shoulder. Then she pounded his chest with her fists as well. She was frenzied. He wrapped her with his arms and drew her from sight. There was no dampening her cries but no one had seen or would see Janna without male disguise. The navigator and his assistant had left an hour ago. Abel had waited for Janna's arrival after that. So Janna as a female was safe and unseen. Her true identity had not been discovered. And the throttle of her voice was diminished by the power of the wind that blew that night. It was just her heart that had been totally battered.

Those beautiful tear-filled eyes of hers blazed even through the liquid's prism.

Then she swished the droplets away from her face and lashes and stormed, "You are worse than Mikilenia! You made me captive to you for centuries. And I gave you the fullness of my passion and my genuine allegiance. And you realized all along, all along you godforsaken thing, that this lie of yours, this lie of omission, was more horrible than the misbegotten act between you and her.

"I can forgive a mistake, even one as huge as sleeping with her. But I can never, do you hear me, never countenance your being so viciously dishonest."

The body of Janna went suddenly limp and he kept her from falling completely. "Could you not have told me? Or spared us this agony? Why, oh why?"

The trembling hands of hers brushed down his pants until they rested on his bulge. She had no idea that she had even done that.

He stepped slightly back in surprise and simply said, "I give you your freedom."

She was not about to have any of that! She needed to share some more of herself with him. But not in a position of indignity and weakness. She raised herself and fronted him, chest to chest. "Mikilenia has suffered in this brazen act of yours! He has suffered for so long. And all along, you, who could have, should have stopped this act. Instead, vile fiend, you rendered me puppet and drubbed Mikilenia again and again in anguish.

"You have no soul! And you give me nothing! I take my freedom because it is mine to take!"

Abel comprehended the irony. She obviously didn't. Of course he had no soul; he was the king of demons. He laughed aloud at this irony but his laugh quickly was strangled by the moan that broke from his throat. His agony was so genuine.

A cold rip of remorse pierced his innards then. He was struck by his emotions as they ruled him so strongly. Why had he not listened to his better self those many years ago? He did have a better self. He valued that; but not enough even yet. He was ancient and it still had not been enough time.

She slapped him and drew her talons across his now bloody cheek. "You and I will part forever. I will try never to set sight upon you again."

He was abashed and humbled. "You are right in doing exactly that."

"Damn you again. I would damn you to hell except that I know that is already where you are! And it is where you belong forever!

"Mikilenia will have his opportunity to convince me that he is softer and more worthy. I have a vague sense that he has learned something since he and his mother entwined. If so, I am his. The trust might be rebuilt very slowly between him and me but he will have my unending effort."

Abel closed his eyes and the entity let his senses surround her. He had just an instant for this before she pushed his seer sight from any part of her body. And what he experienced in this brief and last interior encounter with her was his own remembrances of their longstanding companionship. Had he brushed up against anything of hers after, he would have felt only a bottomless chill. His memories were sweet and they invigorated him enough that he was going to overcome the pain of her leaving.

That pain would diminish but never die. He did love her.

She though flinched and gasped as soon as she felt his tentacles bore into her. She backed up and shuddered as she glared at him. "Do not think that you will ever captivate me or penetrate me again. It won't happen in our unending lifetimes."

Abel longed for her return. She was here but already absolutely gone.

As she rushed away from the earth and back to the moon's embrace, Abel knelt to the hard surface of the ship and placed his forehead on a plank at his feet.

The heaving sea of his remorse drowned out the sea that rhythmically slapped at the bow of his ship.

CHAPTER 22

White Truth

The tryst in the cavern, two nights ago, blinked out in its present insignificance. Janna was bouncing back to solid ground to sound out the once king, Mikilenia. And where was his consort she wondered? Far away or Janna would not have Mikilenia either. She was aware of her own beauty and value and planned to go elsewhere were she not appreciated as she felt that she deserved.

Mikilenia knew her value as he had pined for her and behaved irrationally ever since she left him in the chamber of their royal Annex in the city of Scone. For the first time since she had flown from him, he began to experience an ease creep into him. He had to be rigorously honest with this creature as she accepted nothing less. She was loving and exceptionally steadfast but was scrupulous in demanding the truth in all expressions and utterances.

She was to receive nothing but that snowy white truth from him. The white of his honesty was to be pristine. He desired that now equal to her.

He sensed her nearness to him and all that he was aware of was that he had an opportunity now beyond his hopes and dreams. He was ready to ply her with reasons, if necessary, for her choice of him as her constant partner. He controlled himself rigidly. Only a twitch or two occurred to reveal his blended anxiety and excitement.

Her sudden presence riveted him. He didn't need to ask her, he comprehended, but asked her simply to fill the empty space with words. "You asked and found that it was true, yes?"

Janna's stride ate up the distance between them. She ignored his unnecessary question. And, as with Abel, she took Mikilenia by the shoulders. She did not use her nails whatsoever though. "I will not be toyed with by anyone or anything anymore! Can you convince me that you not only hear me but that you willingly cherish sincerity between us? If you can't do this, I will leave you too. I have crushed my doubts in that regard finally. I will never waver on that again and never settle for less than the twins of truth and trust.

"So speak your truth to me now then. Let me feel it, see it, yes and smell it. My ears will be acute too. You will fool none of my senses if you are false."

Oh this was sweet strength he thought. She was definitely finding her path at last. He was ready to follow suit. So he removed any and all blockages from Janna and became vulnerable to her stalking through his mind without constraint. So be it. This was a relief for him. The torture of first, his secret, and later, his anguish, had pounded him too thoroughly to countenance ever letting it be his master again.

"Look into me. I desire that you do exactly that. It is time that I tend to my healing. And that won't occur unless I have the balm of your trust. So search the most subterranean shafts that you can find within me. There is nothing left that I would not reveal to you now. Find that out now so that you become certain and then certain of us. My healing comes with our union. I am yours."

She began her journey into the freely opened crevices of Mikilenia's mind. Even that he willingly did this for her nearly convinced her of him in and of itself. But no, this time, she planned on being anything but naïve or gullible. So she wove her seer sight into the cloth of his character and history.

She fell into their romantic beginnings on the margins of Loch Fyne. They had been quickly engulfed by their attraction, rapture even, for one another. The silver choker had been passed from her to him as token of their bond and fidelity. Unfortunately, that bond was created in the heat of the often suspect promises of young lovers. It did not last. She spoke pregnancy and his every intention unraveled overwhelmingly. His shock drove him to leave her on the spot. As an inexperienced woman, she too was in shock; the shock of his abandonment when she most craved his presence. But her maturity as she probed told her the obvious. He had not been prepared for fatherhood. He was nineteen then, old enough physically, but still adolescent emotionally.

They did not meet again until their first born was sixteen. And it was only by the purest of happenstance as this man had given up the notion of finding her ever again. And it was in this period of separation that the seed of anarchy and duplicity was planted. While she lived in a city miles away, he had become liege lord of the kingdom of the Gaels which was passed to him at his father's brutal death.

As she rummaged, she began to smell the strong and earthy scent of the entity within this newly appointed king. It was in her hunt then that a vivid scene from his memory came leaping into her. Both father and son were about to be ripped from life by a sorely determined enemy. The son was saved but the father was not. The entity had penetrated the son's interior and with that strength brought fresh energy to the fray. Wildly, the son, Cinaed, Mikilenia now, started hacking away at body after body. His father was not so fortunate and was beheaded.

Janna recoiled at the vision of the father's head spiked through with a sword up to its hilt. That sword was hoisted high for all to see. And see it she did; the stump of the neck was ragged with oozing vessels and rent flesh. The rigor had set in and the eyes were wide open, almost as if in disbelief of his own demise. The sword bobbed up and down and the opposing soldier's spat on, jeered and poked at the once proud warrior.

It was such a cruel scene that Janna's physical body took a step backwards in the horror of the killing.

But it was the next scene that had laid her and Mikilenia low. She hissed as she observed it happening. But she watched out of the necessity of knowing fully and then purging it completely forever. This was the only manner in which she was to be able to forgive Mikilenia his wrongdoing. This deed of his consumed her, this deed only. She comprehended that she would observe all forward of this event but that, though much of his behavior was alien to her, she was little concerned. He had felt bereft and had acted foolishly until this moment.

So she reviewed what she loathed and would never observe it after this.

Mikilenia and the surviving troops had returned in conquest. Though they had limped home with many injured and few in one piece, they had celebrated fiercely and without regard for their exhaustion and their decimated numbers.

The entity coexisted within Mikilenia, Cinaed then. They were a temporary pair, both with senses to comprehend all of their circumstances, all of their actions. Most especially, how could the entity have allowed this to happen? She seethed as she went forward.

It was as she had perceived once, briefly, and she reacted more calmly this time. She used the term calm this time loosely. She had no calmness toward Mikilenia in Catrione's arms. But she did not have sensations of collapse as she had had the first time viewing the incestuous tryst.

The details of their encounter assailed her and she barely found a capacity to brave it.

Catrione was provocative and mead stoked. Mikilenia was attracted to her bold offering. He had been drinking cup after cup of mead too. And the temptation obviously became irresistible to him. He succumbed as his mother took the lead. It was accomplished in a private room and as Catrione sank onto his full and engorged cock, Janna was mesmerized and sickened at the same time. It was unbelievable that his mother had been so vile. And that the entity, immune to mead on this or any occasion, had passively watched the damage be done.

Mikilenia was the least of the three to blame. And he had suffered the most; even more so than his mother. Catrione had the faithful Eumann at her side and their love was not dimmed a bit. Mikilenia had lost his capacity to love and he perpetually brought harm to himself and others for that very reason. Anteekwa was grossly damaged as the emotional consequences spread ever wider! Time for it all to stop!

Mikilenia underwent a lightening of his mind. He almost lost his balance it was so strong. Obviously, Janna was finished and her probe was gone.

"Are you satisfied?" he asked.

She was shaken; but not by Mikilenia anymore. And the wrath that she still had for Catrione and the entity was sure to scatter as time moved on. She, hopefully, was never to encounter the entity again. And she and Catrione had never formed any particular ties. No wonder!

"I am content; as content as I can be after forcing myself to watch that wretched act!

"I do finally forgive you. You have been in pain so long. It is enough. I am yours again."

Mikilenia buckled to his knees and knew that even though he was undead, he was alive again.

CHAPTER 23

Its Unwinding

He had no choice. She was fully fascinated and relentless besides. And this Te Maori soldier had reversed her outlook so irrevocably that Anteekwa poured her happiness out in an unyielding desire to understand him completely. Unlike most individuals, her curiosity began with his culture. Most would have chosen to learn the personal details first. Not so Anteekwa. She was unique in every respect.

She insisted, "Tell me what it is to be Te Maori."

He was nude as she was nude. She leaned in and caressed his cock simultaneously. They had already joined but she had become insatiable in her excitement. She was hardly aware of the expanding column of his lust as she automatically squeezed and stroked him there. His words drove her mostly for the moment.

Those eyes of his fixed intently upon her while he ignored her languid strokes upon him. His mouth smiled and then went serious of a sudden. "Each warrior is well versed in all parts of Te Maori history. Our history created us. We know it well.

"Here is its unwinding.

"Our ancestor's waka came southwest from their homeland to arrive near this very spot where we have chosen to sit. The water over which they canoed was vast and some died in the effort. Those canoes had names. They are revered and were called Aotea, Arawa, Tainui, Kurahaupo, Takitimu, Horouata, Tokomaru and the Mataatua."

She warmed even more to him as he proudly recited each outrigger canoe, one after the other.

"In legend, the father of our people, Paikea, attempting to escape the treachery of his brother, Ruatapu, jumped into the sea and was saved by riding the back of a whale from his island of Hawaiiki to this island. Paikea and his love gave birth to Tahupotiki. His lineage went on to create the tribe of the Ngai Tahu of which I am a member."

Anteekwa yearned to suck on his now thick and pulsing stem of flesh, contrasting pale cockhead flaring, but was even more eager to hear all about his story. So she removed her restless hand from him.

Without distraction, he continued. "We have become the strongest of all the tribes on this island. We conquered and we married and we spread widely. It is a blessing as my people are those who can best care for this land. We have a trade in greenstone that multiplies our wealth and assures our superiority.

"There are others that we have not overcome, yet we intend to without hesitation."

"What is greenstone? And who must you overcome?"

"It is a hard and beautiful green rock that we treasure. The Moriori defy us."

Tongea, Anteekwa's warrior man, palmed a tiny jade tiki carving from around his neck and held it up to his new found partner. "This is greenstone."

She dreamily polished the object with her thumb and forefinger. It had such a smooth surface and an intricate design more complex than that of her copper talisman hanging from her nipple.

"It is beloved and exchanged for mana and passed from one generation to the next. It takes many cycles of the full moon to shape the stone." And those shapes that he referred to became ceremonial knives, tools in the form of chisels and adzes, carvings, jewelry, fish hooks and sewing needles. It was not only beautiful to them but crucial to their survival.

She touched his tattoos that masked his face nearly completely. "Yes," Tongea said, "These are my moko, my signature, and it is unique to me. It did not scare you but it always places fear in my enemy's heart and trembling throughout his limbs.

"Feel my face lovely woman. It is without hair of any kind. My moko is always visible and never hidden. So I pluck the hairs from my face repeatedly. It is effort that my pride commands of me. And I will always celebrate it until my skin peels from my bone as I die."

She loved how adamant he was. It did remind her of Mikilenia. But she brushed that wicked thought away instantly.

She was entranced by Tongea's physical prowess as well. And that brought vivid images to her mind of his involvement in war and its accessories. "How are you in battle wondrous man?"

"I love most what occurs before we clash with our adversary. Peruperu haka is my greatest skill. When we see our angry friends, those who would hurt us, we do a dance with our weapons that are meant to frighten them intensely. And we enter a trance that feeds our courage up and up until we swarm and slaughter the enemy. It is then that we are certain our dance has satisfied our war god."

Tongea stood suddenly from his sitting position. He grasped his long spear and was seized with manic motion. He pounded the blunt end of his spear into the hard earth. He sliced at the air with his free arm in a chop to show what he planned to do to that enemy. At the same time, he commenced a rhythmic stamping of his feet, rolled his eyeballs until only their whites showed, acted out grimaces and fierce facial expressions, hung his tongue out and shook it and all this was interspersed with grunts and cries.

"We shout for them to come straight this way over and over until finally Ahuriri gives a command and we spring forward as one body as if we are a huge stone thrown in the air. It is impossible to imagine even with my individual show of force." He sat then. They were as they had been, facing one another in a cross-legged fashion.

Anteekwa respected his valor and all that went with that. "And your home, have you been away from it long?"

"I have but am expectant that I will be back soon. Our war party has accomplished so much and it feels like it is time to be homeward bound."

He was unable to contain himself what with her rapt attention to his words. That a stranger to his culture was thrilled by its mechanism pleased him no end. "To understand us fully, you need to know these details. What I am about to reveal to you lays the foundation for who we are and who I am as a man and a Te Maori. Home is only a piece of us."

"I sense that there is huge heart within your people. I want to know it all." In her pull to him, she had reflexively stroked his inner thigh and it trembled slightly under her touch. At this point, she was willing to listen to whatever he spoke to her. She heard him but was so entranced that her heart beat rapidly and her womanly sensations transformed his words so that their effect accentuated erotic feeling over intellectual meaning within her.

She was tempted to suck on his never flagging pole before her but resisted the urge again. She chose to show him only consideration. To minimize his fact telling by distracting him hugely was not reasonable. So she forced herself to quit stroking his thigh . . . again.

He settled and continued. "Your touch is wonderful. Your pleasure in wanting to know me, my people, is even more so.

"There is this about us, the Te Maori. We are a collection of powerful tribes with a chief, an ariki, commanding our attention and determining our direction. The senior son of the senior family becomes the chosen one. I am of a significant senior family but have brothers who have greater years than do I. So I am a member of the ruling class and we are the rangatira. My brother Ahuriri leads us. I do not sit in the council yet.

"Lineage is traced through both our mothers and our fathers. We value them both as fully as we are able. Amongst the aristocracy, the rangatira, there are priests who guide us. Some take us to the world of spirits, some heal our ailments and others remember the tales of our society and pass them on so that no one or thing is ever forgotten. Clans appear next in our hierarchy. Those hapu have extended families within them and then there is the small center of close family members, the whanau. Many of these people are commoners but we cherish and protect all of our Te Maori brethren. It is our duty and our choice.

"All may have slaves. It is good like this." His chest swelled ever so slightly and Anteekwa resisted him less and less. Mikilenia was far from her thoughts and was disappearing rapidly.

"The home itself is warm and bustling with activity. The huts are modest except for those of our significant families and the priests. Those dwellings are larger and more elaborate as is correct for those important individuals.

"We love our music and our carvings.

"We love to eat. And the Moa we love to eat best. They don't fly and we catch them easily." He said this without regard to the Moa. That common bird was not to be common for long.

She was gazing at him and had succumbed. She was his and always would be. She severed all emotional ties with Mikilenia in this instant.

"Mana is good and we do all that we can to bring it to ourselves. Tapu is necessary and is not to be challenged. Ever!"

She was consumed. She rocked forward to him and encircled his still throbbing column with her mouth. Then she grasped his sizeable girth with her hands and stroked him hard. He had been waiting for and seeking this from her. He bent to her too and their cheeks touched. He reached for her talisman and twisted and turned it harshly. Then he squeezed her nipple there so hard. His moans reached a frenzied growl. Her moans were as if she intoned a mantra. She ravaged his cock in her passion. She gasped periodically when she ran out of breath. And while sucking him she panted raggedly.

He moved his fingers from her risen nipple to her flooded opening and thrust them inside her. She froze at his movement. Her hips twitched and he pumped fingers into her very deep. His cock was so swollen and ready. It was when her vault quaked of a sudden and then she cried loudly around his white mushroom head that he burst into a release of his own. Her explosion was wildly intense, lengthy and her orgasmic waves engulfed his fingers. He too shot many jets of himself into the deepest recesses of her throat.

Dawn was arriving. She had no idea how to turn him. She was such a novice she realized.

"Meet here again!" she kissed gently into his ear. He could do no other but meet her again here. He just mutely nodded.

She and he parted. And, yes, it was such sweet sorrow.

CHAPTER 24

Boredom Compounding

Filched the Heemskerck's small boat, they had. They had done it just as their watch on deck ended. Late daylight filtered through the thin layer of clouds above them. And three of them paid no attention as the fourth oared the tiny rowboat. Truly, their boredom had compounded while the ships were moored and they were desperate to find amusement on land. They had one lantern sitting between them as they planned on being ready for the dark of the night.

They had been brazen not only in stealing the boat beneath their butts but they had managed to quickly grab a stash carved out of the ship's plentiful bottles of beer, ale and brandy. To bolster their courage, they had found a prized bottle of gin and had immediately passed it around to all. After several gulps of that for the four, they slyly put the bottle back in its original place. It was the slyness of fools.

The gin had caught up with them by now and the raised bottles of the plainer alcohol were putting quite a heavy hand on their senses. But they didn't care a whit and were hoisting drink after drink to their lips. Even the provocateur, the idiot who had suggested this venture, the one attempting to row the boat between lunges at his own bottle, was guffawing and pouring a steady stream of the liquid down his mouth. Most hit his throat but enough flowed over his chin and soaked what was left of his miserably dirty uniform.

The boat wagged back and forth but actually moved slowly toward the darkening shores; movement in a straight line was out of the question though. Not that any of them worried that specific too much. It was uncanny how lucky they were in spite of their disregard for anything wise or reasonable. That they had timed their venture as they did was all that allowed them to succeed. Had Abel been awake, he would have dashed the sailor's plans so quickly and punished them so thoroughly that any rowdy stupidity would not have been considered by the crew on the journey again.

As it was, Abel was pounding the sleep of the dead; or rather the undead. And his second, Visscher was in his cups and oblivious to anything and everything. His snorting snores attested to that fact clearly. Obviously, they had been anchored in the bay for too long.

The four were blessed as their little rocking and weaving vessel seemed to have a mind of its own and, with a last push from the surf, planted its miniature bow into the sands at shoreline. The sudden jarring stop after the lurching movement from the wave's swells nearly pitched all four out of the boat. Each one recovered their balance and staggered slightly through the foamy ankle deep liquid. Had their craft not skidded deeply into the white of the sands, they would not have anything to use to return to the Heemskerck. Even then, they had only a certain amount of time before the sand would release the wood as the tide came in.

No one even glanced back. Their concerns were elsewhere; like maintaining an upright stance as they erratically loped forward toward the forest beyond the shimmering beach. Two carried their flintlock pistols and were fortunate that those weapons remained dry. Between all of them, they had a rapier, a cutlass and several long knives. They swaggered, when not staggering, in their confidence. "Not a blasted soul will stand a chance agin us!"

"Aye to that!" the rest bellowed.

They quieted mostly as they pierced the forest deeper and deeper. The lantern was their only ally as they began to carefully rove through the thickening timber and the spreading overhead canopy. The now risen moon offered them feeble light through the layers of branches and brush. As time elapsed, they found themselves growing more and more spooked. The flickering light of the lantern brought shadows as well. And these shadows created a tableau that was weird and even frightening. The bravado generated by the alcohol was fast disappearing.

The two with flintlock pistols set charges for the ready and surveyed their perimeter.

Their surround was whisper quiet. The only disconcerting aspect really was the unpredictable effect of the lantern on the dark.

Even as drunk as they were, these men were experts at approaching danger. And they had been trained for the surprise of warfare whether it was on land or sea. They intuited accurately a change at the brink.

Suddenly, two other bodies, one a huge bird that slapped and crushed the ground cover with its three toed feet and the other a brown skinned muscular male with a completely tattooed face, barreled toward them at breakneck speed. The hunter panted hard and pounded in a sprint that drew him close to his prey. He had his long shafted wood spear poised to kill the bird. The creature shrieked, darted and changed direction in a blur.

Two explosions rang out one after the other. The Moa collapsed at the feet of the sailors. It had been shot as it nearly collided into the shocked Dutchmen. Those adventurers were suddenly sober and stood stock still as they stared at the dead bird. Then they whipped their heads up as Tongea nearly crashed into them.

The young warrior was nearly as stunned by the four white men as they were by him.

It was only that the flintlock pistols had both been discharged that saved Tongea's life for the moment. The guns were being reloaded as the Te Maori froze at the sight of the bird that should have been his and at the strange colored individuals who did not belong here!

Tongea did what he knew best when confronted with a dangerous enemy; he danced crazily before them and waved his long spear at them.

The seemingly bizarre antics of the burly native prompted evil dramatics from the four immediately.

And neither a word of the Dutch nor a word of the Te Maori was understood by the other.

The pistols were primed and ready now. The balls of the weapons were discharged and their aim was true. One struck Tongea's right thigh and shattered bone and the second lodged in the arm which held the spear. It went flying into the space behind and became useless to Tongea.

He fell to the forest surface, writhing in agony and screeching in disbelief.

The shooters had not intended to kill him right away. It was a bit of sport that they were after. "Quiet yerself now!" A knife tip was placed at the underside of his chin and lifted

Tongea's entire head upward with the pressure of the blade. "Shut up ya bastard!"

Tongea understood the gesture and cruel barking tone. He did exactly that. In spite of his devastating pain, he clamped his mouth shut.

Another blade brought its artistry to his back where the letter x was cut out of his skin. Tongea felt the blood spread over his flesh there. He believed that their next step was to peel his skin from his spine. He attempted to keep from shaking but could not. He was about to die. He was not about to escape this death sentence as he had with Anteekwa.

He would draw himself into his mind and move past the agony. He meant to say not another word . . . ever. Let them appreciate how a proud soldier dies.

"Make him speak! Damn ya speak!" cried one of the men aiming a pistol at Tongea.

"I will have ya show me what I need. Scream. Do it! Or we will have yer balls. And then yer ugly black heart!"

A knife dropped down to his groin and the cold metal made his testicles, his entire body, shrink in a great gasping fear. But he still made no sound.

Chapter 25

Unlikely Rescue

Shadows completely engulfed the horizon and their eyes flew wide open. Anteekwa was horrified and her cry of anguish went out to all the others. All went instantly; even Janna who had desired to never lay eyes on the entity again.

Anteekwa's cry was not a request for aid; it was simply a gut deep response of revulsion. But the enormity of the feeling involved compelled the others to react. And it was later that Anteekwa would find herself utterly shocked and surprised.

None went disguised. Those details were extraneous in this emergency.

Abel walked first into the circle of lantern light.

Pistols were leveled at him in a flash.

As the remainder of the vampire crew followed into that light, the deckhands found snarls that showed Abel no deference. "How is it ya're here, Master Commander? Who're these that walk at yer shoulder? Answer me! We are on land and I takes orders from no man on land!"

"Put those weapons aside and I will spare you. Continue to point them at me and you will be corpses in no time." Abel said this and he stood completely still. Only his mouth moved and his eyes gleamed. The remaining undead planted themselves as if statues.

They had already seen Tongea in their mind's eye and experienced all that he experienced. His silent waves of pain knocked at the inner walls of all of their skulls. The cruelty was despicable and there was not going to be much allowance for either the fact that the perpetrators were crew or that they were drunk.

"Ya don't have any say in this here Tasman." These words were hissed out in menace that was not to be denied. And continued, "Frighten us, ya don't. Go and pretend this was ne'er seen. Or else yer turns come followin. We have the guns and drop ya we will."

Abel laughed a very hardy laugh at the bold words.

That dumbfounded the rogues as they expected their commander to turn tail and run. His damnable party too. "We'll put shot in your arses as ya run; specially those pretty whores a yern. What brings any of ya here anyways? Wipe that look ofn yer face and start hightailin it! Now ya buffoons!"

Scottish to be sure, Abel conjectured quite easily. They were definitely not Dutch; and definitely from the foul gutters of the foulest slums in one of that country's largest foul cities.

Even as Tongea writhed, Abel had to give these scum one last chance. The entity had been developing a conscious for millennia and he was not about to stop now.

"Cease and desist! That is a command!"

"Ya don't command us ya uppity prig!" Two rounds of shot rang out and a rapier and cutlass were thrown simultaneously. Their singular target was Abel and he flinched as the lead balls hit him in the chest and forehead.

The rapier buried itself in his thigh and the cutlass sliced a gash in his ear as it whizzed by.

Abel spun once and then faced them again. The shot gurgled from him; fell to the ground and those wounds knitted instantly. He pulled the rapier from his leg and his leg too closed and the wound disappeared totally. The lower portion of the ear, that which was almost severed, healed too once Abel held the dangling portion against what remained.

The concussion of air was loud as the vampires slammed into the unruly four. Negotiations were over and the last memory for the four was that of their necks being ripped open and their precious crimson sluicing out of them into the gulping holes of the creatures at their throats. There wasn't even time for a struggle. The bodies went limp, complete exsanguination of the hapless individuals ensued and then the fleshy shells were tossed so that the undead could lean in to the poor tortured Tongea.

Anteekwa crumpled over Tongea's body and wept incessantly.

And though he and Anteekwa were lovers no more, Mikilenia had to perform for her. Her sadness ripped at his heart as it did all of them. So he was the first to move Anteekwa aside and thrust his fangs into the Te Maori's carotid. He sucked with the intent of transforming the man into undead flesh. Then his wounds would heal.

Ah, but he had forgotten one factor. And that was why Tongea suffered still. His wounds were bleeding profusely and the blood kept flooding out. If Mikilenia didn't right the situation soon, Tongea would have no blood to feed any vampire.

But it had to be the correct vampire for transformation. There had to be a former connection, even mild, of some kind for transformation to occur. Mikilenia did not know

Tongea at all. Anteekwa was alone in that regard. And she had never turned anyone. She was ignorant of her power to revive Tongea.

Mikilenia grabbed Anteekwa's hair and lifted her keening face to his. "Follow my instructions. Take this man's flesh in your hands and then suck from him. Transform him. Do it before it is too late!"

This jarred Anteekwa as she brushed away her tears and attempted to compose herself. She stared into Mikilenia's eyes blankly.

He simply took the back of her head with one hand and her chin with the other and ground her face into Tongea's proffered slope of throat. "Feed. Feed on him." He screamed it at her.

Her mind clicked and she launched into drawing the warm and salty liquid from him. Tongea quivered and moaned as she did this. She took draught after draught.

Her thirst was slaked finally. She withdrew from his flesh and under her intense scrutiny, Tongea revived slowly. The lead did exactly as it had done with Abel. The raw and gory x cut on his back came together and sank into him as if nothing ever had happened there.

Tongea was undead now. Even before, the demons understood his language. That was their power. And it would be Tongea's too from this night forward.

Tongea marveled at his escape from death. Miraculously, twice spared somehow. And though he was not alive, he was to learn all that there was to learn in this twilight life that he owned. He was thrilled and would never look back.

Anteekwa was astounded at the events just occurring. Tongea breathed and was well. And almost equal to that, she had been aided by those that she thought were her enemy. It had been the most unlikely of rescues by hardhearted creatures. But they were not hardhearted. And she realized that she had done despicable things to them. She had acted as adversary repeatedly.

They all read these notions of hers. Even if they had been unable to peer into her mind, they certainly were able to read it on her face.

Janna reached to Anteekwa. "You have entered our fold. Both you and Tongea are joined with us. We welcome you and accept your astonishment at this new unity. Take it. Trust it."

Anteekwa lowered her head in acceptance for a moment and then they all stood as one together.

They dispersed after.

Janna and Mikilenia retrieved their shelter as did Anteekwa and Tongea.

Eumann and Catrione went to seek out a special place.

Abel rowed what amounted to a dinghy back to the Heemskerck and shrugged when asked about those unaccounted for. "I got separated from them when we went into the woods. I became disoriented. Fortunately, I crossed paths with a native there. He led me to shore and the boat.

"I waited. Not a soul came out of the forest. I shouted their names many times but there was no reply whatsoever."

As soon as the liquor supply was uncovered as short, all nodded their heads sagely. The four had lost their heads from the dark and the drink. Most doubted that they would ever return.

Nor did they care much.

CHAPTER 26

Blood and Triumph

The butchery was not an uncommon thing. Oft times might did make right. Therefore, Catrione and Eumann were content, even with the slop of blood smeared on their chins. But it was licked away in due course as the final remnants of a righteous repast. They gave it so very little attention actually, as no one deserved to be wiped from the face of the earth more than those thugs did.

It was a leisurely stroll. There was much of the night remaining and there was a calmness of blood and triumph between them. The blood filled their bellies and the triumph filled their senses.

"He is finally pleased. It's a mother's greatest satisfaction to observe her child's happiness. And he is my son; my only child. That he has come to the blossom of fulfilled opportunity has stirred me even beyond what I had anticipated.

"This, of all, is the achievement of his that I treasure most. And it does swell my chest to realize that I had at least some feeble part in repairing what I had so viciously torn."

"Your part was what allowed him and Janna to heal her animosity toward your son. Nothing compares with this, not even when you almost single-handedly gave him the Scottish crown by your lineage and by your hot and noble persuasion."

"My part is unimportant except that he trusts me now. Even more significant though is that he behaves sanely and with relish. He is my joy."

Catrione began to realize that she had never felt so light.

Even when her son was a youth, and her then husband and his father, Alpin, sorely mistreated her, Catrione had not realized the strain that Alpin's behavior placed on her spirit.

Her personal eclipse had passed and her energy was returning. She felt as if she would burst. Catrione's countenance brightened even in the shadows and the feeling of elation gave her a midnight glow.

The undead too have beating passionate hearts, and Catrione's heart was bounding within her full-mounded chest. She took Eumann's right hand and placed it over her heart.

"My love, do you feel this thumping here? My spirit is liberated, and my heart beats for you; for all of life. I feel content in this moment."

Catrione began to feel so playful. She looked around to see if anyone was watching, an old reflex when she had been human, took Eumann's hand, crinkled her nose at him, and led him into the rainforest.

"Come my bold lover; come with me into the cover of the forest! We need to celebrate this delight and the abandonment of my once saddened spirit now!"

Eumann nodded his head and a broad smile flashed upon his stalwart jaw.

"Yes! Oh, yes! Lead on Catrione! This time of love waits for few. Run deep into the forest!"

And they set off. They were light on their feet as she roused Eumann further and further by her uncontained excitement. He would follow her anywhere.

She shed her clothing piece by piece and Eumann followed in kind. Catrione laughed as the vines and ferns tickled her skin as she brushed by. Her full breasts bobbled as she quickened her step. The contact of the leaves against Eumann's cock stimulated him and his member began to thicken and lengthen as he kept pace with Catrione.

The moon just barely revealed itself through the lush canopy of the trees as it highlighted the silhouettes of the curled and lacy fronds of ferns. The beards of hanging moss veiled Catrione and Eumann as they settled under the umbrella of privacy the forest provided. It was as if Papatūānuku, the earth mother herself, was embracing them.

Eumann cleared the area and found a bed for them from the tiny mosses and liverworts that grew in delicate festoons and lush sheets on everything from treetop twigs to the forest floor. It was a cushion, moist with dew from the night air. The rainforest locked in the warmth of the day, and Eumann and Catrione felt like the first beings on earth, as they took to their natural divan.

Eumann sat down and Catrione, still feeling playful, gave him a nudge that had him lying down in seconds. She straddled him and on all fours above him, kissed him hard on the mouth. Eumann's eyes opened wide and he let himself enjoy her dominance in their play.

Catrione's tongue was hungry for him; she explored his mouth, finding his tongue and swirling it with her own. He released himself from the deep kiss. He reached up and gripped her dark long curls. He pulled her hair back so that he could kiss her neck. Like so many years ago, he let his fangs grace her carotid, and allowed only the tiniest drops of blood to come to the surface for him to taste the iron salty sweetness of her.

Finding two moss covered palm sized stones, Catrione removed Eumann's hands from her hair. She was suddenly feeling mischievous. She had a particular game in mind.

"Here, hold these above your head and do not move your hands. I plan to give you much pleasure, but if you move, I will stop. Understand?

"Do not speak unless I give you permission to utter a sound. Mind me now." She smiled. But there was a stern seriousness behind the upturned corners of her mouth.

Eager to please and be pleasured, Eumann nodded his head. He placed his hands as instructed. It would be difficult to remain still, but he craved the touch of his love.

Catrione, still on all fours, moved up higher and let her large brown nipples rest above his lips.

"Keep your lips closed. I will tell you when to open them."

Eumann nodded again. In doing so, his lips brushed against her nipple and it swelled into a hard pebble. Catrione gasped.

"Open your mouth and let your tongue lash my nipple."

Eumann followed these orders. His tongue emerged and he flicked it across her nipple. With tongue flattened, he licked circles around the aureole. Catrione inhaled, but did not exhale, as she moved to let him take her other nipple; aching now for his mouth on her. She arched her back and held her breasts as he moved from nipple to nipple.

The longer that she held her breath each time the more sensation she derived from him.

"Ohhh, my love; your tongue is a gift upon me."

Catrione began to move down Eumann's torso. She ran her fingers through the matted hairs on his chest. His nipples were deep in color, so firm and tiny, surrounded with the only puffy soft tissue on his entire body. She sipped at them and let her own fangs barely touch the tips. Eumann flinched a little, thinking that she was going to bite him. She looked at him out of the corner of her eye, as if to say, "Don't move. You know what will happen."

Eumann stayed still, reveling in her power.

Catrione was famished now in her hunger for Eumann. Her breathing was intense and he felt the wetness of her vault on him as she slid down his body even further. She kissed a trail along the center of his abdomen and dipped her tongue into his navel, swirling it around there. Eumann growled. Catrione positioned herself in between his legs.

"Yesss, oh yes! You like that. More my love, I give you more. Hold the stones. Don't move."

His cock lengthened and swelled beneath Catrione and, as she continued to trail down his center, her nether lips parted and she felt the fullness of him against her firm and heated jewel. Some of her own slick creamy dew lubricated the outer side of his cock's shaft.

She had moved down fully and her face was just above his now standing member. The dew on the tip was beginning to drip over the edge of the head, which was velvety to touch and so red. The ridge around was near purple in color and the bulging blue vein pulsed with the blood that engorged and caused his cock to grow even more.

Catrione eyed the seam running down the middle of his testicles and in her passion, ran the tip of her tongue back and forth across that tender area. She cupped her hand around the sack and at the base of his cock, and then began to brush it back and forth softly with her full palm. The dew on the tip was tempting and her tongue could resist no longer.

She tasted the dew and let it slip over the surface of her lips. Lubricated now, they slid over the head of his massive cock and she took most of him into her mouth. Her breathing was shallow and fast; she was panting and getting closer to her own orgasm, merely from fellating him.

Eumann loved her sucking and stroking. He groaned increasingly and Catrione began encouraging his sounds.

"Let me know your delight in my play."

"Oh, Catrione, amazing love of mine. Your lips, your hands, your tongue; I crave everything about you. More! Please more!"

"Eumann, I must have you now! Toss the stones! You are the winner of the game. But I don't care!"

Eumann obeyed rapidly and sat up. He did wonder briefly what the game might have been.

His cock was standing straight up and reached for the night sky. He lifted Catrione. As she spread her nether lips, he guided her down onto his shaft, gently yet firmly, all the way, until he felt the ring of her core close in on his very tip.

He pulled and twisted her engorged nipples and Catrione arched her back as she began to grind down onto Eumann. She held her breasts and thrust them to him to seek more of the mixed pain and pleasure for herself.

Eumann now took hold of her curvy hips and lifted her almost off his aching cock. He began the rhythmic lifting and lowering. Each time he pounded her onto his throbbing long column a little harder.

"Faster! Harder! I am so close!"

Eumann obeyed once more, his own breathing rapid and shallow.

Catrione's jeweled clitoris found just the right spot. There was no turning back now. She responded in an explosion, sending the heat all over her. Coming. Coming. Coming! She shook and shuddered as the ripples of orgasm overtook her.

"Ohh, Eumann! Eumann! Fill me up!"

Her tight muscles clenched on his cock and her toes curled.

"Keep holding me inside you, my love! Yes! Just like that!"

Lifting. Grinding. Over and over. Eumann rocked as he pounded Catrione down onto him.

He began a low-pitched growl as perspiration beaded on his brow. Catrione held onto his strong arms as Eumann began to reach his poised threshold.

Grrrrrr . . . Ohhhhh . . . Yesss, he hissed as the first spurts began to jet into Catrione's vault. Her nails dug into the flesh of his upper arms as she steadied herself on his pole.

So many streams filled her to overflowing and some of the creamy elixir flowed back onto Eumann in a tiny puddle.

They were totally wrapped within each other's arms and legs; a weave of flesh. Nothing could separate them. They were fused and one. Eumann kissed his Catrione deeply. Their heartbeats slowed.

Contented now, they lay atop the moss, enjoying the afterglow, lazily caressing one another. Fingertips tracing over brows, faces and necks, nipples and arms.

The night birds called. The moonbeams shone through, and the sound of the insect's rhythmic hum added to the fullness of their lovemaking.

Papatūānuku had taught them well; embracing them in her forest arms. Now, Eumann and Catrione embraced mother earth and the gifts she had shared with them this night.

Eumann, under control now, peeked into her mind and found that he was supposed to have let the stones loose in his excitement. It mattered not.

CHAPTER 27

One of Us

There was much to learn. And, as before, she was so eager and anxious to absorb all that he was about to divulge to her. Anteekwa had been born and raised on one side of the world but she planned on living down under with Tongea throughout her remaining days. And he anticipated introducing her as his bride to be. Before that was possible, he had to instruct her in their innumerable customs so that all would be proud of his choice of partner. The ceremony would formalize their pledge of a faithful and everlasting bond to one another. It was their way and the Te Maori punished any deviation without appeal or mercy.

"When you were turned, you left your people. I am turned and I will not leave mine. So, if we join in the Te Maori ceremony of marriage, you must be sure of you and me; as sure as I am that you are the one for me."

Anteekwa was ready to be genuinely loved. Mikilenia had never with her and once she discovered that she had felt destitute. Her period of devastation was extraordinarily brief but that was a fluke; an astounding fluke but a fluke nonetheless.

It was simple. Her heart had been knit back together with the golden thread that only Tongea carefully wove.

Her restoration was so powerful that her love for him was instant. She trusted his oath of love to her absolutely. "I left my tribe for love misjudged. I will stay with your clan for love perfected. Teach me everything. I am yours and I am ready."

He held her face upward to his and then pledged his love to her with a kiss that felt unending. "You will be one of us then."

Slightly out of breath, he began.

"It all begins with our idea of mana and tapu."

She was gravely intent as he began. She so needed to understand it all.

"Mana comes first. It is prestige, influence or power; honor even. There are three sources for the mana that is bestowed upon anyone. Some of this energy of authority one can control and some mana are entirely outside of one's control.

"You have no choice over what is bestowed upon you by birth. Your ancestors are everything here. It involves the rank of your parents, their parents, your grandparents. The higher the rank the more certain is a large amount of mana. But rank is not the sole factor either. If your ancestors have achieved something significant or brave for example, mana seeks you out in abundance.

"Your mana in that regard is not known by us. You come from different stock. And the Te Maori, in not knowing, will gauge your birthright mana as being nonexistent.

"We both are undead. That can be disclosed to my people. We will generate no disapproval because of this. That you and I are the same and that we are powerful and ferocious will convince them that mana dwells in you in abundance. The detail of your birth and your ancestors fades in importance."

This was easy for her to digest. She acknowledged to herself that he was a proficient teacher.

"The manner in which you conduct yourself, from the instant that I inform my clan of our intentions, will increase or decrease your mana. Your conduct will be studied and your regard for our rules and laws raises mana up or lowers it down for you."

"What are those laws that you speak of?" Anteekwa was impatient to get to the core of how to direct her behavior successfully for herself and her man.

"Hush, love. I must do this as I see fit to do this. Imagine that you are building your mana by listening to me closely and trusting the order of my speech to you. Questions are for later.

"We have traits that may seem at odds to you but both add mana. Individuals who are humble when it is appropriate but brave and warlike when that is appropriate are given much mana as others sing their praises. Yet these self-same people never sing their own praises! That is one of a number of certain means by which to lose mana quickly. Arrogance is hated by the many and you will feel the poison darts of displeasure bloody your mana severely.

"As creatures of the night, we must never feed on our relations; no matter how desperate. That is grossly forbidden and would drain all mana away! Promise me that you will never resort to that. You must promise me."

"I make that promise to you sincerely and without doubt. It is what I would have done even if you had never told me of this. That will be easy." She brushed the back of one hand's closed fingers gently over his cheek as she said this.

"Mana is forged within us by our group too. The hapu, my clan that you will be entering is an honorable clan. It is well regarded and your mana will grow from simply being a member. If you take care of those other members, look after them in times of need, feed them in times of request or celebration or help with the building of a home, the group mana will enhance the mana that you already possess.

"The gathering of mana is good."

She saw that clearly. It was good but she was still anxious to understand the very specific details as it sounded to her like a very precise system that prevented gross misbehavior. And, in her past, she had been stubborn and unruly. She would check her impulses often until it became a reflex for her to follow the Te Maori constraints willingly. She would do this for Tongea.

Having read her mind, he continued, "Tapu is exactly that. It is a set of sacred prohibitions that dictate our behavior. Tapu is very strict. If an object, person or place is considered tapu, they may not be touched by humans. If they are highly tapu, one may not even approach without grave consequences. Here is an example; the commoner may not touch anything owned by a member of royalty. The penalty there would be death. You and I are considered definitely of the rangitira. So, as aristocracy, we would not want to nor be allowed to touch items owned by the commoner. If that does happen though, as royalty, the only consequence is to your mana. But that is consequence enough!

"Our chiefs and priests are always tapu. The houses which they dwell in are tapu as well. A religious ceremony must be performed before you, or any woman, can enter tapu dwellings. Once the karakia has been finished by the priest, then you may enter.

"Burying grounds, our urupa, and places of death are to always be assumed as tapu. Do not enter those areas ever.

"Private tapu bears its weight on individuals. Public tapu brings its focus to entire communities."

Tongea leaned in to Anteekwa and kissed her forehead. She let out a huge sigh of relief. "Support me in this always."

He wrinkled his brows and so very seriously said to her, "I would never do other."

She kissed his hand and sighed once again.

"Noa is that which lifts tapu from that which is already tapu. Noa removes tapu and gives safety to one and all. A tapu dwelling may go through a noa ceremony so that there is no risk of violating the sacred energy. Avoid these hara, these violations. They bring the wrath of the gods and leave the offender sick or dead.

"We are already dead so we do not fear deaths outcome. But for the sake of honoring and obeying my people, we will abide by these restrictions.

"Only a few facts of mana and tapu left my love. Your patience is adorable. All of this explanation might bore those of lesser constitutions."

They laughed together.

"My people believe that exploring the past is a necessity. Our history tells us of mistakes. And the only way to avoid those mistakes in the present and future is to inform ourselves and learn and not repeat foolish actions.

"Our word is holy. To break our word is to disrespect the heavens. Be very cautious there. Be very careful before you speak." His solemnity had only grown. Even in her power possessed, Anteekwa found her heart beating harder.

"And we build all of our shelters to face east so that the first rays of the sun are observed. That serves our purposes as well. It allows us to realize when we must retreat to our sanctuaries.

"There is much more but this is enough. More might be forgotten."

Anteekwa simply laid her head on his shoulder and rubbed his back in soft and gentle circles.

CHAPTER 28

Once Again

This particular patch of volcanic activity was rather peculiar and was like nothing that he had ever witnessed before. And when they had happened upon this terrain, as he and Anteekwa swept over it, he had been determined to explore it further until he understood its jagged and unruly nature. Incipient sunlight had not allowed him this luxury. Later it was to be; and that later was now.

He had not anticipated that his return would be with a creature not Anteekwa. And he had especially not dreamt, except on dream's edges, that Janna, his forever love, would move in unison with him in this search for their first trysting in what seemed eons. It had to be a place unlike what he had experienced prior. It had to be so pristine that even his seer sight scanned no sentient beings in its cluster of probes. And it had to be magnificent beyond her expectations. This was that, he was sure.

They were at a great height yet. But the scenes below were beheld. Holes in the earth there shot sprays upward. Some came as steam that constantly saturated the air. The odor was distinct but did not extend to where he planned their rendezvous to take place. Some came as more steam but in intermittent spurts that rose taller than the other liquid plumes. And they were both able to hear the bubbling of something thick. The pop-plop sound was not unknown to them. With their abilities, they quickly discerned that it was active hot mud that had collected in small pools.

The ribbon of a spring that flowed from the volcanic maw here was long. And it was much downstream that they landed and transformed. Mikilenia looked askance at Janna. Janna simply glowed.

The water gave off a heat that caused vapors to drift into the night's sky. And the shoreline sloped so gradually and so smoothly down to the inviting ripples minutely cascading over several tiny rocky ledges buried in the channel of the always volcanically heated brook.

They padded softly over the fine grained and warm sand at their feet. She was entranced and her desire vibrated intensely for him. Once again, they would find their delight together.

Mikilenia's craving for Janna was so concentrated within him that the vertical sounds of his blood rushing through him were shrill and penetrating, roaring and hissing like the very geysers themselves. His blood boiled and splashed back into his heart, and repeated the process with each beat. Mikilenia doubted that he could restrain and suspend the urgency of his need for long once fully embraced with his love. His seers mind understood her unspoken words and he saw the heaving of her abundant bosom as evidence that she felt the identical way too.

And it was that signal, with gaze still locked, that they both slow peeled their garments off themselves and dropped them at the riverside.

Mikilenia stood only for the briefest of moments, absorbing the breathtaking view that was his love, Janna. Her breasts were ample and rounded, her hips slender yet curvaceous atop her lithe and agile legs. Her long wavy strawberry blonde hair was blowing in a sudden swirl of gentle wind that was a welcome breeze.

And she took in his rigorous handsomeness. Oh, he had those strong brawny shoulders and burly broad chest with muscular abdomen and narrow hips atop legs of stone. His steely cock reached straight up almost as high as his navel and she remembered instantly the reddened shaft, indigo veins and that head so large and darkly hued. His sack gently cradled his kiwi sized balls. Her desire for him nearly caused her to swoon.

Mikilenia sensed and lifted Janna up above his head with strong hands around her waist. He buried his head in the globes of her breasts and twirled her around and around. His muffled intonations of her name came repeatedly.

She felt little warm droplets between her breasts. They were tears he left for his love.

Janna laughed aloud and fisted his hair, while wrapping her legs around him. She kissed his head and caressed his ears as they began an immediate and urgent feast of love.

Mikilenia felt his own warm dew bubbling up from him and Janna's soft and plentiful moisture against his velvet plum.

He lowered her until both their hot centers met. Mikilenia looked into Janna's aquamarine eyes deeply as he entered her. He was deep within her now and his loins had already come to a boil. His breathing was ragged and he knew that this would be quick.

Janna started moving up and down, and Mikilenia kept the rhythm as he held her hips and brought her down harder and harder each time.

"Unh! Unh! Unh!" she cried. She gasped for air. Explosive heat permeated the two of them. They quivered and clung to one another as their orgasms rocked their melded core.

They merged as their orgasmic melt triggered them to come perfectly, completely, and unequivocally into one. Fused, Mikilenia and Janna would never be separated again.

He took her in his arms and gently laid Janna down near water's margin. Blissful and serene, they laid together. They then playfully rolled into the glistening water that washed over them. They laughed at their spontaneity. As soon as the laughter drifted away, the only sounds they heard were the ripples they had caused lapping at the sands slope. With continued calm, they also heard the sounds of the breeze rustling through the leaves of the shoreline trees. In the distance, geysers burst and mud burbled.

As they were liquid-caressed, Mikilenia and Janna slowed their tempo to soak up every nuance they had so long missed in the absence of their love.

Mikilenia traced imaginary lines over her face. He barely believed that she was really in his presence. Never mind presence, he felt incredulous that she was skin touching skin with him at this very moment. He had to know all of her once again. As long as it took, Mikilenia would touch and kiss every inch of her skin, and he would know her inside and out.

He was at a loss for words, and could only keep whispering the poetry that was her name.

"Janna, sweet love. You have my very soul, dearest Janna."

Janna closed her eyes and felt the slight pressure of the pads of his fingertips on her brows, eyelids, nose and cheeks. His thumb rested on and caressed her lips. She took his hand then, and kissed his palm. Shimmering tears welled at the outside corner of her eyes, and trickled down.

"Man of my deep spirit, my darling Mikilenia, pain once seared my heart, but love healed it completely. You are lodged within this heart of mine without hesitation now. I will hold you there forever."

"Undead as I am, as we both are, I would surely be cast into the very fires of hell were I not to have you spend eternity at my side." Mikilenia's own eyes welled up again.

Janna brushed the droplets away with her thumb. She placed a finger on his lips and whispered, "Shhh."

Their words blessed the marriage of their souls.

Mikilenia scooped up Janna in his arms and moved her further onto the soft sand. For now, they paid no mind to the white glittery particles that adhered to their skin. The couple was too deeply involved in their own embrace.

Their lips sought intimate contact and Mikilenia brought Janna's face close to his. He turned his head ever so slightly and plumbed her with his kiss. Parting her lips with his tongue he explored that mouth that he had so many times before. She met his tongue with her own and the swirl of romance danced.

Janna touched Mikilenia's face now. Her thumbs brushed his lush brow and cheekbones; she caressed his ears that were hot to touch with his excitement rebuilding. Her lips followed the path of her touch.

She turned her head and proffered her neck to him. Mikilenia planted the softest of kisses on her carotid. There was no need for even the tiniest drop of blood to be let. Running her fingers through his hair, she guided him lower to her aching nipples.

Her breasts were like large passion fruit in his hands. Firm, yet with the silky delicate skin. His cheek was somewhat coarse from his beard growth, and she loved the little bit of pain-pleasure it gave her as he swept across this soft flesh and delighted in her. Her aureoles still held that raspberry stained color and her nipples, substantial and hard like the guava cherry, yearned for his suckling mouth. Mikilenia cupped a breast, and swept his lips across her nipple and whispered "Oh Janna." before opening his mouth to taste her.

Janna's neck arched as she thrust her breasts upward. Her passionate desire for all of Mikilenia became further pronounced. She longed for the intensity of their coupling once again in short time.

Mikilenia pressed even closer to Janna's face and their kisses took on urgency with the heat surging again between them. His cock had revived; it grew and Janna felt it with all its sandy hardness against her.

While the sand particles provided a sparkling effect, Mikilenia found them to be slightly irritating to his skin and he didn't want to provide even the slightest pain, physically or emotionally ever again to his love. So Mikilenia lifted his sweetest Janna once more and cradled her in his arms. He waded into the slightly warm night blue water up to his waist. He lowered Janna into the water and bathed the sand off her tantalizing skin.

She in turn, stood, moved a slight distance closer to the shore and knelt to wash the sand from him.

His cock lengthened and thickened at her touch. She smiled as she removed the sand. Janna stroked Mikilenia's cock and felt the veins pulsing in her hand. She was positioned there to do what she loved. She lifted his cock from the water and let her tongue lash up and down the length of him. Flicking around the tight rim and swirling as she glided to the very tip. Mikilenia's knees buckled slightly with the excitement he felt.

"Janna, sweet Janna. I want you again this instant. Now my love!"

He kissed Janna ardently, holding her close to him, her face in his hands. She gripped his buttocks and pulled him close to her. He felt her very heat against him and knew her excitement met his.

Now, only their feet would shimmer, as Mikilenia shook out his white linen shirt and placed it on the sand. He laid Janna down so that her hips and shapely ripe buttocks were resting on the cloth.

He took his place between her legs.

He caressingly spread her legs at her knees. Her nether lips opened of themselves revealing their pinkness like a fresh cut guava fruit. Her jewel in the center was red and polished. That little nubbin of flesh created such desire for him, Mikilenia could no longer resist.

The dew was dripping profusely from his cock now, and he aimed it at Janna's clit, rubbing the dew over her flesh. Janna moaned and lifted her hips, ready to take her lover.

He lifted her hips more, spread her ass cheeks wide and plunged himself into her vault; staying still only for a moment to let the sensations of their joining be felt throughout each of them.

He stroked with his entire length, finding the ring of her center. It kissed the head of his cock each time he pushed a little deeper inside her.

Off in the distance, the mud was seething and popping. The geyser was building just as Mikilenia and Janna were building. The fumaroles were steaming.

They didn't notice. All they knew was that of their ignited force.

Janna rocked her hips against Mikilenia, and he lifted her even higher to make contact with her reddened and swollen jewel.

"Yess! Oh! Right there! Again! Again!" Janna hissed and her fangs showed slightly as she reached the crescendo of her passion.

An orgasmic groan escaped her lips as she rose and clenched Mikilenia's cock with spasms of her exhilarated pleasure. She cried out his name, "Mikilenia!" Her fangs showed fully in their gleaming beauty then. Her hot passion was thoroughly revealed.

The groan, her fangs, the vacuum grip and tightening grasp of her vault around his cock, sent Mikilenia further and further, higher into his own flight to exquisite pleasure.

Pumping harder and harder into Janna, Mikilenia emitted an extended low growling noise that grew in sound and intensity. His mouth opened and his own fangs arched fully as he roared in upsurge of his climax. Spurting and shooting his semen repeatedly into Janna, covering the walls of her vault with his elixir of love.

Spent and exhausted, Mikilenia sank into Janna's arms. They meshed as one, again.

"I love you Janna, utterly."

"As I love you, my Mikilenia. You are returned to me and that will forever remain."

The night sky was beginning to show the first inclinations of light. Mikilenia and Janna had little time to take any further respite there.

Transformed, they took to flight. Brimming with joy now, their soaring took on an ease that surpassed all else. Mikilenia swooped under Janna and came up on the other side. She followed in kind. This time, she went with Mikilenia, side by side.

And in spite of their play, they stayed just ahead of the encroaching light; almost as if they dared it to catch them.

The coffin at the Heemskerck was no longer her destination . . . ever again.

CHAPTER 29

Ancient Abomination

The repercussions of their ancient abomination drew larger and larger circles around them all.

If they had known anything about evolution, and those mechanics did not discriminate between the living and the undead, they would have comprehended that she was an accidental failure of the genes of the combining cells to replicate accurately.

Even as a vampire, she sensed her difference on some level always. She was mutant and a mutation. Her parents had refused her presence in their lives. She had been abandoned and had not experienced a mother's or father's love ever.

It was nine months after the crowning of the Gaelic King Cinaed that the then controversial Catrione labored long and hard with Eumann close at her side. It was the year eight hundred and thirty five anno domino. They and their server were silenced as the larger surroundings took in nothing; the bowels of Dunadd Hill Fort, the dungeon room with Catrione atop the table of torture did not allow for the escape of sounds whatsoever.

Only these three were privy to the pregnancy.

Catrione was loath to give birth but had no option other than to suffer both the physical and emotional pain of it all.

What had happened? The two had tried to untangle the mystery for nine months.

The midwife, not Badb, who had not moved to this castle with the rest of the entourage, hovered around the pregnant woman and waited anxiously for the delivery. Normally so calm and proficient, this blessed midwife was anxious only as to her intuitions here. She felt disquiet within her deeper gut and that was never a good sign. But other than the strenuous and painful aspects of the flight of the fetus through the birth canal, no obvious signs portended anything out of the ordinary. That didn't fully help but she continued as if assisting two vampires to have a child, alive or undead, was an uneventful operation. For her own safety, she was not about to reveal this to anyone . . . ever.

Eumann was gravely disappointed in Catrione. Not only was there no consoling her but she was beyond adamant that she cut the growing thing from her belly so that it could not take breathe. And to insure its death she spoke the desire to take a knife, any knife, and slash the tiny creature, wrap it in a cloth and then light the bundle afire.

Eumann was not having any of that and when persuasion had no effect on her attitude, he was at her side at all times. He guarded that growing fetus like it was his own child. And upon the crowning and arrival of the newborn he planned on maintaining his wall against her seer sight. This was a first between them and he hated the secrecy. But he would not have the newborn harmed and had already designed a strategy to satisfy each and every one except his love. And he was determined that she would be ignorant of the fact.

Catrione panted and pushed. Her waters had not yet broken.

Until now.

The gush of a light pink fluid flushed from Catrione's opening. It swept the table and then fled over the edges onto the huge squares of stone beneath. The midwife server, the doula, rushed in with cloths to wipe the still spreading serosanguinous flood. More leaked from inside Catrione. Once sopped up, the event was ignored and the doula encouraged Catrione to breathe and push, push and breathe.

Eumann, as the astute teacher that he always had been, was ready to aid either woman in whatever fashion he was told to do. He had seen births before, had even had one baby bundle drop into his outstretched arms and then had been profoundly moved by the first squall of the child. It had paralyzed him and the child had been quickly taken from his arms but he was never to forget that precious moment of naked life meeting the presence of the world.

He held Catrione's hands as she cried and whimpered on the table's now slightly sticky surface. Contractions were mounting and the pain that accompanied them was growing in force and fierceness. Catrione moaned out, "I do not want this to be happening to me!" She clenched her hands into fists, pounded the table with them when she could slip them from Eumann's grasp and hissed the exclamation over and over.

Eumann finally restrained her hands and stared into her eyes. "This too shall pass and we will be the much better for it." He uttered it so calmly and softly. But the words brooked no argument or resistance from his love. He had supreme strength and he was applying it with a focus beyond fury.

Catrione grimaced with the reoccurring pain of childbirth but did not say another word nor strike the table again.

The doula had slid the pregnant vampire by the hips up to the bottom edge of the table and then sat her upright. There was no device within which Catrione was able to place her feet in though. So Eumann was shouted for by the doula. "Get on your all fours and let your love place her feet on your shoulders. I will straddle you and handle the birth. Can you do that?"

Eumann kissed his partner on her forehead lightly and quickly; then he strode to the end of the table and swiftly got down on his hands and knees.

Meanwhile, the doula stood over Eumann and massaged the outstretched belly before her.

A piercing pain lanced to the core of the already agonized Catrione. She cried out and panted irregularly. "Push to my count." The doula was in charge and the pregnant woman pushed exactly as instructed. "Now bear down and hold it. Breathe. Again. Yes. That is well. The head is crowning. Continue. Bear down and hold it. Do it, harder. You can do it."

The vampire screamed and then the baby slid quickly into the doula's arms.

The doula lifted the tiny bundle, automatically forgetting the mother's disgust with the pregnancy. The bundle squalled. "Open your eyes and see your daughter."

Eumann was still poised on his all fours.

Catrione vibrated in her hatred and screeched that she would never open her eyes to this daughter of hers.

The stunned doula suddenly remembered. She hurriedly reached for the flaxen string dipped in the astringent of the woad flower. It was to tie off the cord still attaching mother to daughter.

Eumann began to rise but was not fast enough. Catrione ripped the fleshy cord from between her legs, blood spurted and the two were separated. The air was thrashed wildly as she transformed into bat form and winged through hallways and then launched herself out of the first exit she found. The sky was salvation for her in this instant.

And she would pretend that the horrible product of a horrible entanglement did not exist.

Eumann initiated his plan however. He had not quite known how to remove Catrione from the scene but she had provided the means herself. He smiled at the doula.

The doula was aghast and understood nothing that was just now happening. Her fright shoved her hard and she thrust the newborn into Eumann's arms. Her tongue cleaved to the roof of her mouth and she ran for the door without a backward glance.

He peered down at the daughter that was not his but whom he valued immediately.

He spied the tiny fangs that gleamed at the corners of her mouth.

She was undead without a doubt. That two vampires had created a child was impossible. But here she was.

Eumann departed to find those who would cherish and care for her.

CHAPTER 30

Tiny Fangs

Eumann stood there. He felt drained as he looked about. The room looked more like excruciating torture and murder had been committed within its walls, rather than a suffered and laborious birth. Blood was dripping from the table and spattered everywhere. The placenta stuck to the floor in a gloppy heap.

The birth of this baby had been excruciating for Catrione. She departed from Eumann in such angry haste, her undead heart full of enmity, and now he was left holding this babe. It was exactly as he had wished.

Eumann looked down at the bluish pink bundle in his arms. Her eyes, for the moment, black as coal, appeared as if she were looking quizzically at Eumann, trying to figure out who he was and what was going on. Her tiny brow wrinkled and she winced as if in pain. Eumann sighed, knowing in his seers mind that, yes, there would be much suffering for this child. How it would end, he saw not that far into the future. And as the undead, why should it end at all?

He cradled the babe with affection but knew that he could neither keep her nor care for her. All he could give her was a name. He chose Marsaila for her. The appellation meant having much strength, potency, and power.

She began to shiver and squirm; she fussed loudly. Eumann swaddled her in a piece of flaxen cloth found close at hand. The tight swaddling was reminiscent of being womb bound and comforted her briefly. She began to wail as only a baby reflexively can for her mother's nipple. She had no need for a mother's breast to nurse her though, as blood was her exclusive diet, Eumann tapped his fingers. He contemplated how he would feed this wee one. In the tapping of those fingers, Eumann was struck with what seemed a clever idea to him. He bared his fangs and lanced his own index finger to draw the red oozing liquid for the vampire baby's first taste of blood.

He inserted the very tip of his bleeding finger into Marsaila's tiny bud mouth and she suckled immediately, as if latched onto her mother's tit. Her own diminutive hands held onto Eumann's strong hand and her miniature fangs felt like pin pricks as she continued to suckle and draw more blood.

Her petite belly was full. There was no more fussing, and Marsaila settled into what Eumann hoped was peaceful slumber.

His prior plan was now in action. He had not spoken with those he had chosen as her much more permanent caretakers but was confident that there would be no issue in the delivery of the beautiful babe to these women.

He had already settled on Peigi and Jinti, two young women who were in service to Cinaed Mac Alpin. They had a simple dwelling but it appeared comfortable. There was a root cellar that Eumann surmised would be the appropriate place to hold a coffin for her day time repose.

Though undead, Eumann would smooth the complexities out for them in his explanation and then their natural urges would take over. Eumann both saw and intuited that.

A vampire born would grow as normal children do, save for the topsy-turvy vampire needs of day time sleep and night time activity. She would mature to the age which would be the perfect blush of ripeness and then cease to age evermore. Peak beauty's infinite pause was just another of the sweet demon-gifts given the rare naturally born undead.

Still long before the sun had arched yet again into the sky; Eumann took to the streets with the sleeping little Marsaila cradled in the crook of his arm.

He arrived at the home which Peigi and Jinti shared and knocked as he called out "Greetings ladies. Open for me! I have a waddled waif. Be quick."

They recognized his voice as part of the royal entourage and bid him welcome as they opened their door and their home to this tired, angst ridden silhouette and the babe he carried as well.

Eumann's chest rose and fell as he heaved a heavy sigh in the telling of the sordid tale of incest between their king and his own mother. Peigi's hand flew over her mouth, incredulously and Jinti collapsed into a branch framed chair when they were told that the wee babe was indeed a vampire. He lifted her rose colored upper lip and revealed her petite fangs. He explained to the women that Marsaila could only drink blood for sustenance and that she needed to be protected from daylight as well. They understood the tales of the vampire but were now intimately engrossed in its reality.

The two did not refuse Eumann's pleas to take care of this innocent newborn. He went through the wherefore and how so in the manner in which she should sleep. There was a rustic covered wooden box in the corner that, with

Eumann's help, they lined with soft sheep's wool over straw. The box was placed in the root cellar, where Marsaila would avoid the noxious light of day. It would be challenging for the ladies to turn their days and nights around, but they already had affection for Marsaila and were willing to do what was necessary as they became mothers together for their little vampire child. After all, there were two of them. And while one served the royalty at night, the other would serve their marvelous Marsaila.

Eumann swore Peigi and Jinti to secrecy; citing that Marsaila must never know of the incestuous deed of copulation that led to her birth. The women agreed. They for certain never wanted the words of such malevolence to cross their lips.

Little did Eumann know the extent of the insight that this small bundle held. So how would he have been able to discern that oaths were pointless?

He held tiny Marsaila, reluctant to release her to their care. Eumann lifted her up close to his face and let his cheek brush hers. She turned her head reflexively and tried to suckle his chin, and he jumped when he felt those tiny fangs prick his flesh there. Not enough blood flowing to feed the hungry baby, he bared his fangs and lanced his finger again. Once more, Marsaila drank from him and was satisfied after a few minutes.

Peigi and Jinti stood wide eyed and with mouths agape. Eumann assured them that they would not have to feed Marsaila in this fashion. She required blood however, but it did not have to come from their slender fingers. Animals of various sorts would suffice. Offer freshly killed creatures and Marsaila would naturally suckle.

Their mouths closed but Eumann was not quite sure that they were relieved.

Again, he lifted her to his face. They seemed to lock eyes as he whispered to her, "Little child, you should have an eternity of life ahead of you. Be well and grow. These women will love you as mothers. You are a piece of my partner, Catrione, and as that, I love you as my own."

His eyes, glassy with a veil of incipient tears, closed; a lone tear escaped and trickled down his cheek.

Eumann kissed Marsaila on her forehead and then relinquished her to Peigi and Jintis' care.

He could stay no longer. The heartache was almost unbearable. He bowed slightly to the two women and took his leave. Once outside he walked a few steps, then transformed and flew off into the night in search of his only love, Catrione.

Peigi held the baby and Jinti went to the door to watch Eumann depart but he was already fast and far away.

Jinti looked at Peigi and wondered aloud.

"Oh my! Oh my! What to do? What *are* we to do?"

Peigi was calm and reassuring when she answered Jinti.

"Dear friend. We will love this tiny creature, babe that she is. We will do the best we can to raise her as our confidante, Eumann, has asked. Just look at her. She is not at fault for the appalling conception that brought her into this world. Let us do what we can to make her time with us as decent as we can."

As Eumann instructed, Marsaila slept in her makeshift coffin in the root cellar during the day. She did not move or moan; vampires were without conscious capacity at all then. The two were the ones who slept fitfully as they awoke intermittently and listened by the cellar door, just in case.

They became quite adept at finding blood to nourish Marsaila. For the most part, she looked and acted like a typical newborn baby. At least, that is, until she opened her mouth.

Through the dark of night, Peigi and Jinti sat and took turns holding her. They marveled at her petite features. Marsaila was gorgeous; even with those tiny fangs.

CHAPTER 31

First Blush

Despite being undead, Marsaila grew like other children and had many qualities that ordinary children possess. She was inquisitive and precocious. As a young child, the biggest challenge she faced was to accept why she had to be asleep in the day and awake in eve's shadows.

Her vampire abilities and her comprehension of her undead existence developed and deepened as she matured.

By the time Marsaila was in her late adolescent years, Nineteen, Peigi and Jinti had eased away from the sheltered environment that they earlier had provided her. She began to find her own independence and acquire some freedom from the double set of arms that protected her.

Marsaila struggled with her own physical and emotional development; for in truth, she was not just like the other young adults . . . As her body began to develop and mature into a young woman's form, she too felt the urges that prick within; those that often alarm as its first blush colors the cheeks of maidens.

Undertones of her undead essence were awakening as well. Her hunger for blood was increasing. She felt the fierce inexplicable urge within her undead spirit to transform and to fly, testing this awkward ability repeatedly until it became more familiar to her.

Her soul grew more tormented as the evidence of her vampire nature emerged. Marsaila took on a dark persona and in all behaviors appeared very restless.

Marsaila had been in repose and was just beginning to rouse and awaken. She stretched as much as the confined space of her coffin would allow. She was in total darkness and kept returning from being partially awake and drowsy to a dreaming state.

There was giggling and laughter emanating from the upstairs. The laughter came from Peigi and Jinti, but there was also distinct male laughter coming from the overhead bed chamber. Did neither of the women have royal duties at the King's Quarters this eve?

Marsaila was just coming into her seer ability and cocked her head slightly to one side and then back again to try and take in the overhead images. Her mind's eye took her to Peigi's bedroom. There she saw things that she had never witnessed before.

This was no dream.

Save for the laughter, Marsaila may have thought that Peigi and Jinti were in harm's way. But it appeared that what was happening to each of them was thoroughly enjoyed.

The women stretched out on Peigi's bed were completely naked. Jinti faced away and Marsaila took in the rounded form of Jinti's buttocks. Peigi was on the other side of the bed, and between them, a man. They giggled and called him Will. He was tethered, both his wrists and ankles bound to the four corners of the bed by what appeared to be leather straps. Oh how the lasses giggled.

Marsaila was riveted, wide eyed and laughing not a wee bit.

The man, Will, was restrained and Marsaila assumed was not in any pain as he smiled and encouraged the women in their bawdy behavior.

Jinti leaned down and let her wavy curls brush over Will's chest and abdomen. Peigi bent across him and kissed Jinti for what seemed an eternity. Peigi's locks were draped over Will's hips and the base of his cock.

When their lips had ceased touching, the women took to kissing and caressing Will's muscular midsection. Their fingers slid through the hair on his chest and caressed his underarms and upward. They kissed his lips and he responded, offering them more tastes and a searching tongue. He tried to move, but was rigidly held in his spread eagle position.

Marsaila began to feel warm inside. She too was responding to what seemed like wild antics above her. Curious about her own arousal and what might come of it, Marsaila continued to watch the ménage intently with that special power of hers.

Will wriggled as his lovers' hands and faces went further down his firm body. Each of them caressed his inner thighs as they moved their hands closer and closer to his groin.

What was this tube of red, sticking straight out and pulsing? Will moved and it began to rhythmically climb and thump against his belly's narrow trail of fur as it became longer, harder and purple tipped, reaching towards his navel.

Peigi fisted it at the base and squeezed Will's cock hard. His breathing became ragged and Marsaila thought she heard him groan and growl.

Marsaila was feeling an ache expand between her legs. She could barely move. Her right hand found its motion and moved to cup the cleft and aching nubbin of flesh there.

Her heart was beating harder. She pressed her hand tighter at her crotch; the ache did not stop.

She concentrated on the sensuality and lustiness. She was feeling confused but had to continue seeking. Through her thin gown she pinched what were now firm and expanding pale nipples. Each squeeze expanded the exquisite ache between her legs.

Above where Peigi was clasping him, Jinti had grasped Will's cock and began stroking him upward, crossing over the top and then stroking downward. Every time she crossed over the very tip, Will would buck and moan. A pearl of dew formed there and Jinti slid her palm over it to lubricate him and make his flesh slick.

Peigi continued to tighten her grip at the base of Will's cock and bent it downward toward his legs. When she did this, Will moaned very loudly and tried to writhe.

Marsaila, seeing this, began to get hot and her hips were squirming and her legs clutching in what little space they had inside that coffin.

Will's cock was throbbing with the stroking and squeezing. Peigi and Jinti breathed hard as they worked their sweet, sweet magic on his velvet skin.

Peigi's free hand found the center between her legs and she began to rub herself in small circles. She clutched his cock tighter as the circles grew faster and faster.

Jinti moved herself against Will's leg and her own jewel, wet and hot, made contact with his knee. She wriggled against that knee, finding the right spot to grind her bud against him.

Marsaila's fingers separated her nether lips and found her own burning and swelling center. Her finger tips plied both sides of her tiny knob there and trapped it, rubbing her fingers up and down, back and forth.

Peigi leaned down to lick the dew from the head of Will's cock and he jerked, crying out.

She continued to lick him and to compress his thick and nearly purple shaft. Jinti continued to pump him hard, over and over and over.

It was when Jinti twisted his massive erection that Will could no longer hold back. Twisting, pumping, stroking, licking and sucking pulled his taut cord into a fiery release.

Spurts like a fountain burst from his cock, shot after shot, and Will growled loudly as his torrent seemed like it would never end.

Peigi inserted two fingers into her opening and clenched them, crying out in her own climax. Her hips moved in time to Will's spurts.

Jinti hunkered down against Will's knee, and in a minute or so, bent her head down as she moaned and moaned a soft growl, coming in waves against his skin.

Marsaila watched. She heard the sounds and the panting. She heard her own breathing and the sound of her own voice as the paroxysms started from deep within her. She hissed and felt her fangs emerge in the spasms of pleasure under her hand. Her undead heart, alive in this moment, was pounding in her chest.

His pearlescent cream had flown everywhere.

Peggy and Jinti untied Will and fell against his body. His arms wrapped around them. His cooling come caressed the seams of where their bodies met.

Marsaila could hear their muted sounds and sighs as her throbs slowly abated.

They never heard her climb from the coffin as Marsaila, fully awake now, stepped into the darkness of night that was her day.

CHAPTER 32

Stealth Creature

She was the first to see Marsaila standing in the doorway. Jinti inhaled loudly and that sound, along with her panicked countenance, signaled to the others that they were not alone.

Marsaila turned on her heel, but not until she had passed on an expression of aggravation, even anger, at the culpable trio.

Peigi, Jinti and Will tumbled over one another in a clumsy effort to retrieve their clothes. The glee and giggling had frozen in midair and all that was now heard was a quick scuffling search and then an even more rapid shuffling of material over somewhat sticky and resistant skin. They were finally able to loosely apply the material over shoulders and hips.

"Was she watching?"

"I didn't realize the time; the hour is late. Of course she roused! How were we so careless?"

"So she heard our foolishness as well?" That needed no reply at all.

Will had listened to enough of the women's emotional sputters. Now, only caring about his needs, he grasped Peigi by the hair and tipped her head back to kiss her hard on the mouth. He took Jinti's face in his hands and the kiss he planted on her lips made a smacking, squishy sound.

"Ladies, so full of flame and heat, I have enjoyed our play rather much. But it is time that I leave; and leave immediately. I bid you good evening."

And with that, Will exited quickly and recklessly. What else but that he stumbled over a broom that had been dropped haphazardly when he had unexpectedly arrived. Marsaila observed the witless Will's near fall. She rolled her eyes at his imbecilic behavior and then mirthlessly watched him trip once again. Back on his feet, Will scurried off into the dark.

Inside, Peigi and Jinti straightened themselves up. Rumpled skirts and bodices were smoothed down, albeit crooked, and unkempt hair was pushed back into place. Marsaila, who was outside yet, focused on them once again with her seer's vision and took a not so guilty pleasure in sensing their squirming anxiety.

Jinti was the more perturbed of the two. Peigi really wasn't at all. She was annoyed and irritated mostly.

"What do we say to her? How do we explain?"

"We say nothing, Jinti. Our pleasure and our actions are just that, our business. In any event, I don't know what Marsaila comprehends about what she witnessed. We have yet to teach her of sex after all."

Jinti shook her head. "I don't know. I really don't know. We must be more cautious in the future. We will impress that fact upon Will too."

Peigi sighed, still irritated. "Jinti. Stop! Think about it no more. Please!"

Marsaila went back inside to confront her caretakers, but not before kicking that fallen broom. The corner of her lip turned up with her recollection of Will and his stupid look as he careened to the ground on hands and knees when he tumbled over the crooked wooden handle.

Peigi looked at Marsaila from the corner of her eye and Jinti settled her eyes upon the stones of the bedroom floor. She was not about to glance at Marsaila in her moment of shame and uncertainty.

"I have the ability to see things! You are aware of that, yes?"

Jinti rotated her head side to side. She was ignorant of Marsaila's true undead capacities. That domain had always frightened her. Peigi just hissed her irritation in Marsaila's direction.

"I saw everything."

"Everything?"

"I heard it all as well.

"And I experienced it all without leaving the confines of my musty, dirt filled, damnable wooden coffin that has always served as my bed. Could you not have found a more comfortable repose for me. Do you care?!"

Peigi turned to Marsaila. "Our business is our business. Our affairs are ours alone. Do you understand that? You could have averted your senses. We will not apologize or feel shame. It was your choice sassy lass! Do you hear me?

"And how dare you damn the efforts that Jinti and I made so that you would thrive. That you did not have luxurious accommodations is a trifle. We performed our all for you!"

Marsaila sailed on as if she was deaf to what Peigi had just uttered. "Your raucous laughter and sweet enjoyment of your lascivious tryst wetted my curiosity too much to resist the temptation. Can you tell me you would not do exactly as I did?

Marsaila continued, "I am near an adult as I can be. After espying the two of you with that clumsy man, I am initiated and I am more than near. I am an adult. And I will thank the two of you for that."

Jinti gathered that Marsaila was none too happy about being exposed and becoming an adult who was now aware of sordid play and spent passion. So the older woman breathed and responded, "You are certainly a young woman. You learned much in a most awkward fashion. For that, I am ashamed. We shouldn't have played here. We didn't realize that you might notice our pleasures with Will."

Marsaila flipped her black straight hair. She had no tolerance remaining.

"Long ago was the time that you should have informed me of my birth, of my difference. You are late with that as you are late with explaining my body's ripening. And with my visionary powers, I already know of the circumstances of my first squall. But you two should have told me anyhow. You would have had you genuinely loved me!

"I want to hear it from your lips now. Prove that your love for me is greater than a silly alliance with a man who partners with my whore mother and who also has a passing respect for my so easily fooled and naïve father."

Peigi replied steadfastly, "It was our pledge, our oath, and we will not break that oath; even as you say that you comprehend your origins."

Marsaila advanced upon the two. Jinti whimpered. Peigi did not flinch.

"Our love for you, Marsaila, is shown in our tender and careful raising of a beautiful child who is but briefly angry for the moment."

The young vampire snarled with Peigi's words. Jinti cringed but still simultaneously uttered, "We love you with all of our heart. You are our precious Marsaila."

Even Peigi had the slightest quiver when she spoke to her adopted daughter. "We are your guardians. Do not go chasing after phantoms and those who left you behind. Forgive yourself. Forgive the past. Let it alone. And let us love you. Because that we do; we love you fully."

"Agh! I want you to tell me, from your mouth, you and Jinti, what you are aware of in that horrible dark pool that was my birth. It is my birthright to hear it from your lips. I will have no other! And if you maintain your oath," she growled, "I will never believe either of your sincerity ever again!"

To which Peigi replied, "We won't speak of it for you or anyone. Our pledge, our honor, is holy. You will not draw it out of us."

Jinti wrung her hands again, not knowing what to say. She reached out to touch Marsaila, but the girl recoiled and pulled back as if she were being stung.

"Don't touch me! You both are craven. And this is final proof of your cruelty and lack of love for me! I would gash you both right this moment if it were not that you did, at least, raise me."

Peigi hushed and Jinti cowered. The shadow of Marsaila grew large on both women.

Marsaila's temper was flaring so rapidly. She pulled her own hair and pounded her fists on a table, and shouted, "You will not defy me!" Each word was carefully spaced and said with the burning emphasis of the sincerely deranged.

Peigi reiterated, "The truth will neither be revealed through me nor Jinti. That decision is final! You need to find acceptance in our stance."

Marsaila screamed, "Never! Never!"

She pushed over a table in her tantrum and headed out the door. The table spun and then flared with fire. But only Peigi and Jinti saw this.

The broom was there at her feet of a sudden; waiting to trip her like it did Will. Marsaila stared at the broom in her fit of anger and instantly the normally inanimate collection of straw and wood began to move of its own accord. It levitated and began to spin. It spun into a whirling blur and began to smoke. In moments, the broom was nothing more than ash at her feet.

Her fury had caused this and she felt the knowledge about her capacities expand. Her strength could be infinite. Vampires did not have these abilities. She must test this revelation.

She began to run. Her anger fueled her energy. She then flew, not quite knowing her destination. When she was by the shore of the lake, she froze. She peered out over the tar hued water. An idea coursed through her equally darkened mind. And it was a storm of a notion.

Marsaila stared hard out over the water, and rotated her head in a circle. The water started to churn around and around, and a spout formed, rising up from the lake. She was awed and then ecstatic.

What more power had she hidden deep within her tormented spirit?

Marsaila's fangs erupted and glinted in the midnight shadows. She tossed her head back and susurrated a loud animalistic, "Yessssss!" It became evil laughter, then grotesque cackles as she realized what power she already possessed.

"Yesssss!" This became her signature.

She transformed into the stealth creature. She whipped the heavens with her huge wingspan. She left Scotland and all that she associated with that detestable country. She never looked back. And her wish was that she never return.

And what of that wish?

CHAPTER 33

Finder's Dance

She became the finder of those she deemed lost souls and that dance had presently carried her through approximately eight hundred years. She had been her parents' shadow for that span. It had been easy to discover their whereabouts as Eumann had told no one of her existence. And Eumann himself had seemingly forgotten the episode in the dungeon's chamber and then her existence completely. So they did not block her seer sight whatsoever and even if they had sent their probes in her direction, she would have handily brushed them aside. And this meant that she remained anonymous even as she comprehended their every move.

She had motives for remaining patient in obtaining her revenge. She hated her parents for having deserted her. Her father was less guilty because he was ignorant of her birth. Her mother was despicable and Marsaila seethed when she thought of any mother despising her own blood enough to forever leave a defenseless being to its own devices. The cruelty of it, the anger generated within her, gave rise to her extraordinary powers. So, she had to be very careful in recalling her early childhood events. Otherwise, she might ruin the world. Eumann, her savior then, had not even given her existence a genuine fare thee well. Once she was deposited, she was dismissed. He allied with her mother forever after and was scarcely better.

So what were those patient motives exactly? She had etched them in her beautiful hide so that she was not to forget them easily. It was simple. She hankered for some indication of that spark of love for her within their breasts. She waited at length to observe anything heartfelt regarding her or her existence. This was her mother and father after all. She had to show them mercy if it was at all possible. They had created her. She felt caught in that web; the web that neutralized the anger momentarily in the anguish of her wanting to be coveted by those that, yes, she still did love.

Her continued yearning was likely to have no good outcome. That notion knotted tightly in the deeper material of her soul. Yet she held on.

And her trauma went so far that she had been continuously listless in either passion's focus or verve. She was virgin and had bypassed all opportunities for lovemaking. She had so many pursuers but it was a realm of her life that fell flat. Love was a phantom everywhere for her.

Where had her meanderings, that trailed their meanderings, taken her?

She had crossed continents and had traversed from one half of the entire globe to its other half.

And where had this shadowy enterprise moved to? And what were the events that had unfolded during this enterprise? She was amazed at both the where and the what. Since she lived forever, the when held no real interest for her.

Eumann had been her primary target from the beginning. His peaceable and calm attitude amongst the undead left him without some of the shields that the others had. So, in taking the path of least resistance, she inevitably probed him fully and first.

The formation of Scotland had also seen the breakup of the pack of the undead. And she had had to follow the disparate parts, the frayed circle of her significant relations. It took her to all corners of Europe and its outlying territories.

Her father was the most obvious physically for her to locate. If she followed the crown ruling the northern British Isles, there he was. He wore that crown as Cinaed Mac Alpin and was king of the uniting territory of Scotland. He had joined the Gael region with the Pictish region and its amalgamation became Scotland. He was a very powerful monarch and was beloved. His queen, Aiobheean, was more beloved miraculously. She was fair and serene.

Serene that is until her royal partner involuntarily bared a secret that was vile and she, Marsaila, was the product of the ignoble act. For this king, the once Cinaed, was Mikilenia. This was her father and he was stripped of his heart when his life love departed him. And that Aiobheean was the one who was now called Janna.

Names had a way of shifting often in a vampire's existence.

The king had remained king until he accomplished much for his people. His natural death was really not. He rose from the ground grotesquely and went in search of the one who played upon his heart and soul.

The queen remained on the fringes so that she might be near generations of her offspring.

In this round robin of seeking and pausing, her mother and Eumann had discovered the king, Catrione's son. They sauntered through the provinces of their homeland, winged over water's expanse, trooped across the mainland of Europe, met many adventures and then returned to embrace Scotland once again.

The source, the core, though, began with the entity. That creature was difficult for Marsaila to probe. He was the vampire Father. His name was hallowed, his power and will was done and his kingdom had come; a kingdom that was initiated by a brother's murder and another brother's condemnation. She probed this amorphous energy nonetheless as she possessed powers that were unique to her. She was a mutant vampire; unless she had her own offspring, the likes of her might never be duplicated.

She was privy therefore to what occurred next. And the scene morphed from familiar territory to territory of a continent that was alien to her. The entity had led and the rest had followed. They had flown over vast oceanic waters and arrived in the domain of the Cahokia. As Marsaila learned, they were a people in dire need of a forceful leader to carry this huge city to survival and a bountiful longevity.

The complexity of changing alliances within the undead mob was ever occurring. The entity had found a home within the body of the city's valiant leader and the prior queen desired to partner with him. She and he turned out to be inseparable. Marsaila's father, mother and Eumann were close on the heels of the first two to arrive. Her father seethed at the sight of his once love consorting with another. Her mother and her mother's cherished Eumann faded in importance. They stood by the entity and were consulted occasionally but it was a pallid experience. The sweep of Scottish events had captivated them; this did not.

Her father continued his huge pout; a tantrum of the heart that made him irrational at his best and profoundly destructive at his worst. And he entrapped a native of the city to abide by his wishes. She was his lackey, beautiful though she was.

The spectacle, the mess of emotions and behavior, transfixed Marsaila often. Maybe the absence of connection was better than all of this. But her emotions would not let her believe that truly.

Once Cahokia's fortune was found, the whirling bursts of individual reformation pounded down upon their story.

Her father and the lackey, Anteekwa, disappeared into the clutches of the land to the west.

Her mother and Eumann departed to catch Catrione's son and aid Mikilenia in his hope for reconciliation with his truest love. Catrione was successful in this and this knowledge caused Marsaila to kneel, tremble and become extremely sick.

Where was her mother's consideration for her? It seemed only for her son!

The creature that her father pined for fled when the entity left the chieftain's skin. And the entity was pitched into a semitropical environment that was the place where they all congregated now.

And there had not been the remotest flicker of emotion from them for this still bereft child.

Her patience was at a breaking point. And the dark skies began to bunch and gather.

CHAPTER 34

Water Spout

Her frenzy of grief and anger was taking an epic and uncontrollable form. The anguish she had suppressed for centuries was spinning away from her and she wept for all that had been and was about to be. The spinning energy whirled toward the ocean's expanse that surrounded the outer perimeter of sharp coral where she stood.

She could bear her clothes no more and ripped them from her body. She appeared as a mute alabaster column thrusting upward from the reef where her feet were rooted. Her soundless scream filled her lungs and thrust her breasts further forward. She bared herself to heaven or hell; she didn't care which.

What had been calm space was frothing and whipping. The rotating circle of wind that she was generating, some intentionally, some not, vibrated and expanded.

As a sailor for all of his adult life, Abel was intimately familiar with the plethora of storms that beset this part of the global sea. It was her liquid formation that Abel sensed as soon as it began to develop. It was enlarging but was the strangest water spout that he had ever witnessed.

This was no ordinary cyclone. The mechanism of psychic discernment that had ripened into a reflex, used

185

only as needed, was needed now. And what he assessed left him baffled. Though a warmer season was approaching, these dangerous spouts typically massed above the water months later. And that was because the spread of salt seas had not yet been heated to the level that was necessary for this churning wheel to exist.

And the properties of the approaching atmospheric churn were unique and not believable. But there it was. So where were the bolts of lightning flash that always accompanied these storms? There was no heat to condense the tube's air into massive cloud shapes. He felt a strong and gusting wind but recognized that the funnel was approaching with a speed that was rapid and supremely ominous. Most cyclones lumbered so slowly. And especially without the ocean's heat required to increase the velocity, this should not be happening.

There was not even an eye in the midst of all the turbulence. No quiet air at all. The still center was absent; movement outdid everything.

But the most alarming quality that Abel experienced was that his seer ability only reached a certain point. He visualized the storm but saw nothing coherent past that happening. He pressed his eyes tightly shut and both he and the entity labored mightily to go into that unknown.

Bah, the demon king responded, why the need for an understanding. The wet monster was about to rip the ship to shreds and sink both vessels most assuredly. Let others worry the insights. It was absolutely time now to rush to the aid of those in need.

He was paralyzed though. Even the entity's brutish and angry half was helpless to create the smallest of steps. A force was squashing him and planting him to the ship's deck. It was maddening and like nothing that he had ever dealt with before. Even his lips lay slack.

He also understood that the rest of his cohorts were planted in their positions of the moment as well.

And then he heard a scream, more screams, that drowned out the noise of the storm. The sound was shrill and piercing. Now he simply wished to place his hands over his ears to dim the endlessly repeating shrieks.

And Marsaila was not about to cease. And she was no longer silent either.

She bore her bosom outward and tipped her head backward. Her din had grown into the expression of love's denial and she was no longer in doubt about seeking the revenge upon Catrione and Mikilenia that they so deserved.

Whatever had shackled her truest and most vicious emotions for her parents to her insides was being released in howls of pain and demented torment.

The rise and fall of her so porcelain, nearly illuminated, sumptuous mounds would have been so captivating had she not let loose the serpents of the medusa within her. Her power was vast and it shuttered the power of the entity.

The impossible incest had produced the impossible creature. And that creature was Marsaila. And all the world was about to kneel before the onslaught that was her hate and her vengeance. Her parents were to be the first to feel the wrath.

When she stopped screaming, she felt the incipient delight of her primacy and was not capable of containing a rough hissing laughter that seemed to vibrate the sky above.

The evil bird of a mammoth vile pleasure in pounding down upon the vermin who had scorned her forever fluttered its wings and pecked at her sexuality. Finally, except for the one occasion with her guardians, she felt the itching sensation again between her legs. It was not to be ignored as it pulsated more with every passing moment.

She did not shift her torso whatsoever.

But she did lick her lips and cupped her large mounds and hefted them to her mouth. Her tongue snaked out to each swollen, pale nipple. Once having aroused herself more fully that way, she then sucked on them hard. Her mounds were that big and her nipples had surged long and thick as well.

She was not done, not even close. She roughly squeezed and then pulled on her lush and giving tips. She twisted them until the pain inexplicably shifted and her loins caught fire. Her hands went immediately to gently swipe at her belly and then swept down to her thighs' apex. She leaned back and moaned. She let the moon's light caress her round about every portion of her delightful body.

The glossy and slick crease at her opening was running rivulets of lubrication. Her fingers swam in the warmth there. She took her thumb and pressed it down upon her almost pristine bud and hoped to ease her passion for a moment. She wanted this to last. But instead, the pressure caused a bigger and more urgent throb within her.

Her opening quivered for touch and she lanced into her tunnel with two fingers and her thumb still lodged against her clit.

She trembled in weak kneed fashion and spread her legs the widest. But she was not going to come until she had accomplished giving her gift to her mother, at least.

Though sexually focused, she managed to wrest her passion away enough to locate Catrione and Eumann. They had found hiding in the forest after their fervent encounter and then had leisurely sauntered down to the shore on the bay this night. And Marsaila pinned them most assuredly to the sand of that beach now.

Marsaila redirected the path of the cyclone and angled it away from the bobbing ships. She forced it to race to bayside and capture the two in its circle of violent agitation. They resisted being sucked in with every ounce of their undead strength but the witch was far superior and overpowered their struggles. It was a trifle to Marsaila.

"Mother, my dearest mother. Do you recall your child? It is that very child here to return the love that you so lavished upon me." Cackles pinged back and forth inside the funnel.

Catrione whirled along with Eumann. They both overheard the diffuse voice that floated through the center of the storm. It was the torments of the damned to hear her spawn mock her. The spinning paled in comparison.

It was her destiny Catrione knew. Eumann had released the whirlwind and it was bound to engulf them.

Were there miracles in store?

CHAPTER 35

Bright Enemy

The disorientation was beyond the imaginable as the two were hurled in circles round and round, sliding up and down within the differential pressures of the wicked plume of liquid. They were incapable of recovering any bit of stability, let alone find their way through the agitated and viciously shrieking mass surrounding them.

Their only possible salvation was their use of the psychic powers that defied all outside elements. If not their salvation, that flow of words swiftly injected back and forth gave them desperate comfort and the tiniest sliver of hope.

"Transform, transform my love! Regain your wings. I will do the same. That might give us capacity to flap away from this danger." Eumann's probe was fierce and stunned Catrione into instant activity.

Primal senses and a wingspan that was massive allowed them to right themselves against the battering, stinging bullets of rain. They attacked the wet and exploding darkness with the power that two of the undead held between each other. And they darted into the wet sheets together.

"Together Eumann, we do this together. I will not separate from you ever. To be impotent, lost and despairing is not our way!" Her seer's words screamed this into his brain.

"Never separate! Heave to the outside with me!"

They banged and flung themselves, wings beating the air furiously but were thrown back each attempt. And it did not matter their direction. They were caught among the impassable sluicing power of Marsaila's water spout.

And Marsaila shivered in delight at the impending ecstasy that would soon ravage her body. It was beyond even Marsaila to quit thrusting her wedged fingers in and out of her sweet, sweet center. She uncurled her thumb and lashed at her clit on every upstroke of her fingers.

Her moans were gaining strength and even the quietest of them echoed beyond the whipping racket of the menacing funnel that held her mother and her lover trapped and in place. Her powers were vast. She had created one storm and now was creating the same within herself.

The rapture was overtaking her ability to control all that she had created. In one brief instant, she recognized that she was on the verge of losing all control as her orgasm was about to sweep over her. She could not wait for the demise of her mother as it turned out. But what she released to the storm while she still had conscious sense was a momentum that would spin that cyclone for the sufficient time required.

She only managed that last aware action as she was thoroughly sucked into the upsurge of her pounding fingers and strumming thumb. She was her own instrument and the aria that was her passion had passed a threshold and was rushing to a huge crescendo that would bring all of her senses down to her female core. Her moans became hot groans and she spread her legs wide and then squatted down without losing balance so that she felt her fingers and thumb all the more.

It was lush and her body and mind bent only to the impending orgasm.

Abel and the rest were inadvertently released. And, as the sun taunted the horizon and light of day was imminent, they had to scurry for their burrows that sheltered them from their bright enemy.

And it was this bright enemy that now fast approached Marsaila and the helpless vampire duo.

Marsaila was so involved within herself that she paid that fact no heed whatsoever.

She arose out of her squat and arched her Venus mound forward as if it were a weapon that she brandished and aimed at the horizon and beyond. Her entire body began to quake and vibrate. She was saturated with passion and craved her release. The throb was intense and the movement of her hands was now a blur upon her; she continued to press for even faster motion.

Her breath tore at the air surrounding her as she panted and heaved with sensation. Her seemingly polished globes protruded from her torso magnificently. The curve was huge, the sway was hypnotic and the pendulous fall of those breasts were perfect. The raw power though flared from the now nearly crimson color of her thumb sized nipples. She was truly a wanton and possessed vampire creature.

The heat laid its red coloring upon her chest, her neck, face and ears. Her eyes were hard closed and trembling in the anticipation of the violent wave certain to come upon her any moment.

Lightning bolts snapped and crackled in proximity.

The hot and urgent wave of her desire began within her tormented bud, flooded over her entire body and finally crested in the interior of her seizing tunnel. She rode her fingers and then she writhed upon them as if they were a huge cock driven between her legs.

She was delirious. But even as she craved another surge she did not indulge. She burst into winged form and flew to her refuge before the slaughter of light came to her.

Eumann and Catrione were delirious to find their own shelter but were exhausting themselves in the effort. There was no give here. It was like being wrapped in an undertow that refused to relent. Their bat form had proved to have been as futile as their human form.

Catrione was the first to recognize what was and what would be happening to them soon. She sent these words to Eumann, "Turn back into human form my love. It is hopeless and I want to see you as the beautiful man that I have loved and cherished forever."

Eumann watched as his so loved partner blossomed wetly into the appearance that was so common and lovely to him. Before she was able to twist away from him in the tidal pull of the storm's interior, he changed instantly and clasped her hand tightly. The soaked creatures bobbed helplessly but did not let go of one another.

"Whatever our fate may be, relax into it. And be assured that I have loved you once, twice and infinitely." Eumann let his muscles loosen and his resistances dissipate. They continued to clutch at one another's hands with a full determination for fingers to embrace fingers regardless of the circumstances.

"It is what I am doing my love. Let us go into the void together. Our love will anchor us always."

Except for the funnel shape, there was not a cloud in the sky. The yellow orb rose steadily and its rays shone down upon the land.

Though this event was instantaneous, it was timeless for the vampire lovers. They felt the stretch of their skin as the definition of their bodily form became unrecognizable. The stretch pulled on them until it became unbearable. Soon they became a mass of somewhat linked molecules. And suddenly, their molecules imploded and burst into flame. The ashes were awash in liquid and whisked away in the stormy stir. But their hands had been blasted into ash that contained molecules of them both.

What they saw in that fragment of time was the visage of the master, lord of the cosmos. His face felt warm and the light of all colors flashed into their eyes. Even the darkest color glowed.

CHAPTER 36

Fascination and Fear

The hum of his Te Maori fascination and fear was in the air and starkly visible as he gazed in horror at the oncoming whirl. He stood upon the very outer perimeter of their pa, their fortress on the hill, and as their sentry, had an absolute obligation to rouse all warriors. His voice was shrill and of the time tested signal. It was heard far and wide. Immediately so many rushed from their mats, placed their strategically located flaxen belts, with weapons attached, around their waists. They needed no clothing as they were strong and confident of successful intimidation by all their traditional means. And their muscular nude forms and frightening tattoos always made the enemy cringe.

And that enemy, whoever, would surely cringe again.

The sentry jabbed his long stick towards the sky as all of the males gathered round. It wasn't difficult to see what it was that was agitating the well-respected warrior. The sky may have been dense and dark but the movement that approached was not to be missed. And the gusting howl was escalating and heard by each and every one now that they were all awake and alerted to the danger. The wind pressed against their exposed flesh in staccato bursts that propelled them slightly backwards.

But the challenge of the cyclone made these fearless clan soldiers even more defiant. They would take their lead from the reckless bravado that they observed from the ones on the beach that Tongea had mentioned to them once. They were closely related to Tongea's woman, Anteekwa. The long dark locks shifting and wavering in the breeze of the woman in the distance were of the same raven shade that Anteekwa owned.

The beach was being violently roughened into a swirl of mixed water and viciously blinding sand. And this was only the effect of the very margins of the cyclone. The pair suddenly was able to bend down and swipe fingers and forearms at their eyes. In a flash, they were on their knees with heads tucked to their chests.

The Te Maori chose to give support to this seemingly brave pair. They began their peruperu haka, their thunderous war dance, ferociously to their own chant and the rhythmic vibration that the storm brought to the ground. The grounds quaking simply added to the pulse of the clan warriors synchronized movements, mantras and long spear thrusts. They were determined to frighten their foe even if that foe was nature herself.

These men leaped in unison with their legs pressed under their bodies. This frog hop, performed flawlessly and one identically with the other, built the excitement and confidence. As Tongea had shown to Anteekwa, they thought to add to the fright of their adversary by simultaneously contorting their faces into ugly expressions and harsh grimaces. The coordinated dance went even further with long and savage tongue thrusts, the wagging and shaking of those same tongues and the very frightening rolling of eyeballs to only their whites.

They alternated their chants with whoops, grunts and cries.

And they punctuated it all with the waving of their knives and spears.

They did not break their ritual stride even when they saw the unbelievable; the pair on the beach had miraculously morphed into creatures that no longer had human form. The wings of these massive creatures beat hard upon the air and they lifted rapidly upward but were smacked down by the atmospheric crush not just once but many a time. It was also obvious, even from the clan's pa, that these creatures were totally disoriented and not aware of their state or form. They ultimately were not able to hold on to their bat shape and were left exhausted and in their human guise.

It was then that the gigantic maelstrom sucked the disabled pair to its twisting bosom. They shimmied in their torture and then stretched in anguish upon the sand. That was when they vanished and seemed to exist no more. They had been swallowed whole.

The dancers leapt with greater and greater energy. It was all that they could do for the helpless individuals that had pocked the beach until only instants ago. Tongea had spoken of them as allies and allies they were considered then.

As they escalated their speed, it became more difficult to hold to absolutely synchronous movement. And finally, inevitably, several warriors broke from the pattern of all the others. They had slowed and this was horribly ominous.

In that moment, they all stopped and beat their long spears and other weapons on the sloping surface that they had been traversing slowly.

Some rose up and began beating on their chests. Their power had been successfully challenged. They were feeling the loss of those called Catrione and Eumann. They were feeling their weakness and this was not permitted. Their energy and confidence was not to be wasted. None would have that.

Their singular leader, Ahuriri, indicated to them that they follow him back to their clan fortress. It was there that he was planning on telling them of what they would do. And this venture would be fruitful and would counteract the setback that had just been experienced. And his inferiors turned as he turned and maintained their energy now that there was a possible outlet for victory.

When they reached their clan fortress, they remained standing as they did not want to let their vigor dissipate by sitting and talking. So, their chieftain did not plot plans with them. Instead, he told them in the shortest and most efficient manner what they were now about to go do.

Once told, the chants rebuilt, the taut energy of each man escalated and they surged as one down to their sea bound craft. They would ride the tide in front of the cyclone and arrive at their destination without harm. This was what Ahuriri mandated and he convinced the rest that they were about to clash with rivals that would capitulate. And in that defeat of those others, that outside threat would be extinguished forever.

This was the grand and glorious venture that had been sought initially. And their chieftain, wise beyond the knowing, had found a means and a way to snatch defeat away and bring the spoils of the conquering hero's back to their own homes.

The waves were wild and high but as they paddled fiercely, they managed to separate themselves from the whirling funnel in the sky. As they continued to paddle, that same funnel shrank. And it was not that they coursed over the waves so quickly but they could see that it was that the violent air now stood still. It did still spin though on the ribbon of sand behind them.

With further strokes of their paddles, the storms roil subsided. And then calmness returned.

But no one's paddling ceased.

And the women of the clan who saw it all too, with daylight glistening on the tide that lapped at the shore and on the sands that were warming swiftly, went to that seaside area. There were troughs dug into the sand, dunes blasted into flatness but nowhere, nowhere, was there evidence of life of any kind. Even the flecks of ash that had come from some mysterious source were barely visible.

One woman bent to a fuller flake and touched it softly. She did not want it to crumble. She let it go and watched it drift and rotate quietly back down to the sand.

The Te Maori women were humbled.

The Te Maori men were never.

CHAPTER 37

Only Invincible

As dusk dawned for the swarm of vampires in despair over the decimation of Catrione and Eumann, they sought out Marsaila. They were now privy to her machinations. She had allowed their seer sight to reach into her when she mindlessly delved into her orgasm. But as she roused too, she was as unconcerned about that information spilling forth as she was about their united powers. She presumed that she was beyond their control whether they acted singly or together.

As her recognition of her powers grew so did her arrogance. She would slaughter them. She could find no charity in her ruined heart for any of them. They were all vile and she was to have her way with them; a bit of torture here and then a bit of torture there. She laughed giddily at the idea.

A tick of sadness at so much death by her hand came and went so instantly that she was almost mystified as to what emotion had just flashed inside of her. Whatever it was, she swept it aside in the anger that truly moved her. All of those weaker feelings, sadness, remorse, shame, guilt or even compassion, were despicable and she would not acknowledge her own there at all. So, she stomped on those softer regards ruthlessly.

She was not only invincible; she was pleased about her wickedness now. The cloth of evil deeds was beginning to fit her well.

It was inevitable that the faceoff between the adversaries was to occur exactly where Mikilenia's mother and her lover had lost their hold on existence. Mikilenia's desire for revenge necessitated that Marsaila find her last breath there. Janna was equally definite in her fury at the monster that had crushed her own mother. And Marsaila's presence reminded Janna too of what had spoiled the love that she so cherished again; a love lost and then miraculously recovered.

Anteekwa and Tongea automatically rose to protect those who had become her allies since her once companion had saved Tongea an instant before his demise. There was nothing that she would not do for them. And she had a premonition that if the others fell before Marsaila, she and her Te Maori love would be next.

Abel did not need to marshal any forces at all. All waited at the water's edge and Abel met them there.

Marsaila provided them the confrontation that they seemed to demand. She would give her father a chance to beg for her mercy. And once that he had, she would annihilate him as cruelly as she had her mother. And then the rest would follow; even the entity, the oh so pitiably powerful entity; pitiable in that she would dash him to bits shortly. She smirked and envisioned his surprise at the yielding to her superior will and then dying with sheer shock coursing throughout a final wavering essence. And shock was the last sensation that would engulf the abhorrent being.

She lusted for that instant. She found that she was not capable of slowing her juices down now. All was ecstasy for her as she reigned supreme.

Just to tease the gathered fools, she fluttered down gently to stand before the onlookers. They encircled her and she didn't trouble herself a bit about that. She simply turned until she was face to face with her sinning father, the son of her mother. And she was willing to be gracious enough, fleetingly, to allow him to speak first.

His posture told her everything. She did not need to use her psychic abilities. He was all atremble she noticed. His rage must be monumental. Let it be. Let him expose that wrath and then she would smash it with her own dominant ire. She had an infinite amount of that.

"Loosen your tongue madman. I am your daughter."

Mikilenia restrained himself physically but barely. "You killed your own mother! You killed my mother! She had transformed since those olden days. You never even found a first word with her. You put her to death; and her lover too. He was a creature like us but never meant harm except to feed his belly. And that he was compelled to do."

Marsaila grinned. "Oh, she heard me. That she did. She knew who came for her."

Mikilenia spat blood at her feet but continued.

"And I have regretted my loathsome act for centuries. And that was even without the knowledge that a child was born out of her and my union. It was not supposed to have been possible; you were not supposed to have been possible. I have never wiped the taint of that act from my heart or my mind. And now, to know that a cursed child has come of it too, damn me to hell!"

"I will have not the least bit of difficulty granting your wish my father. Hell is where you belong. And now to find your feelings for me as your cursed child, what else would you expect me to do?" She smiled leisurely as she said this to him.

Mikilenia began to lunge at her but Abel clapped his arm across Mikilenia's chest. The younger resisted his urges and fell back.

"Wise of you to restrain him Abel. Or should I call you something else? Entity perhaps?"

The entity remained hidden behind the spirit that was Abel. This was how the ancient one chose to initially approach this dangerous undead woman. Her power was titanic and she had to be assessed calmly. Out of that, a plan for her destruction had to emerge. Let Abel take the lead for now. This was not the moment for the entity. Not yet.

"Call me nothing, you bitch! I see your poison but I also see your uncertainty." Abel snarled that but did not move a muscle other than his lips. His stare bored into her.

She swept his words away with a brush of her arm. "There is no uncertainty in me. You have been too long the strongest of the undead. Once I took my first breath, I ruled everything and will rule you in this confrontation. It did take me a short while before I fathomed my unlimited capabilities. Once I understood, I trailed hot on your path and anticipated my vengeance.

"And it tasted sweet to me to watch my detestable and uncaring mother blast into ashes. Her lover was unimportant. I shrug when I think of his ashes. He never saved me. I would have saved myself!"

Abel tempered himself but still lashed out, "Your bravado is shallow."

It was then the entity realized the breach between her present arrogant stance and her deeply concealed heartbreak and ambivalence over the loss of both of her parents. Abel had shown him the way inadvertently. He looked into her then and saw that she did care!

Marsaila's pride in her gifts made her stupidly careless. She was neither blocking her adversary's seer sight nor was she paying particular heed to their thoughts either. They were weak and they would succumb.

The entity recognized that speed was paramount; and then that all acted in concert too! She had to be caught unawares and then be overcome swiftly and with every ounce of combined undead energy that all could muster together.

The bolt of thought, the demands of his plan, pinged through the brains of his partners; and that included Janna with her own ambivalence toward the entity. All were needed!

As Marsaila laughed triumphantly, the cohort's probes rushed toward that opening into her buried emotions. The strength of their joined probe overcame her resistance to her warring emotions. It was there, and only there, that she was weak. Their probes penetrated well and fully and were made vivid to the beast before them. The probes enlarged the sense of despair until it was so vast that it could not be ignored anymore.

Mikilenia's daughter shook suddenly, fell to her knees, wept and rubbed her forehead in the sand. She was horrified at herself and her sense of joy in the killing of her mother. She was wailing at her father, "I just wanted your love, her love. Where was your love, your mercy?"

The others stood inert as she bent prostrate before them all and continued wailing. The sand scraped away skin enough to cause her forehead to bleed.

Hours passed.

Marsaila was bereft.

As the sun tendered itself to the horizon, Abel, Mikilenia, Janna, Anteekwa and Tongea departed so as to shelter from the light.

When they found safety, their last images were of Marsaila reaching to the yellow orb and finding only her ashes there.

CHAPTER 38

On Their Own

The threat was gone but the need to be away from the killing ground was brutally overpowering. The rift between him and his mother had loomed for so long but complete healing had been at hand. Her gift to him, which brought Janna back into his seeking arms, had been more than appreciated. He acknowledged it as an overture, an offering, of sweeping love from her. And it had smoothed all of the roughness away. She and he had found simple joy in relating as undead parent and child.

And that was why Mikilenia spoke of departure. This land held too much that had been sullied by his mother's death. His emotions were stark and Janna embraced them as if they were her own.

And some were. Though she was hardly impacted by Catrione's death as Mikilenia was, it had been an unnecessary and evil act. Most especially, she burned to remove herself from all of the physical reminders of the conjoining of mother and son. Marsaila's presence had defiled everything that existed here in this place.

Speech was being wholly subsumed by their ever enlarging talent with psychic communication. And it was within this silent language of the maturing vampires that they shared their glance and Mikilenia understood instantly the comforting message of her palm tenderly lying upon his cheek. He recognized her agreement with him, and a calming consolation with her hand's action, in an exit not only from these newly perceived graceless shores but a leaving of ship's burdens behind too.

She had needed the ships when she had required the entity's passion and dominant hand upon her bosom. That she no longer remotely sought. The necessity of that bond had vanished and she did not repent the change one bit. Her fortune now relied exclusively upon a mutual happiness with the male beside her.

The gently pressing palm that touched his skin started a smoldering that pitched forward from that moment on. She had initiated his excitement without any but an innocent intent. He was incited by her caress nonetheless and smoldering heat was evident. Its escalation was inevitable and he reached for her as she reached for him.

The blood filled kiss was lethal yet so soft. Her subtle swoon caused her to lose her breath and pant gently for air. His pulse quickened and his tongue darted for hers. That touch too blanked her mind except to their tip to tip contact. She was unconscious to the increased labor that her lungs were involved in. He tortured her even more by following the rise and fall of her lush chest easily with the pinching of her continuously swelling nipples. He pinched them through the thin material that covered her voluptuous mounds and then had the sweet audacity to grasp her top and pull it above her flesh. They kissed and he returned to not only squeezing her taut, thick tips but twisting and pulling on them as well.

He dropped his fingers down to her slick and gleaming cleft. She was so excited that her thighs clenched and unclenched awaiting the entry of his fingers. He wove them into the hot glove that was her vault and the weave became circular and then high pressure strokes to her deliciously sensitive spot, middle and top inside. Her fluid was gushing for him. She tightened her ass cheeks, released them and then moaned more intensely with each passing minute.

His own column was nearly as large as it would get. He was staggered by her response; he had always been. This was his paradise, his home.

She tugged his head to her heaving huge breasts. She crushed his face to her cleavage and he was forced to remove his fingers from her as he fell onto her hot padding. She writhed and wiggled underneath him and clutched his ass with her nails biting his flesh. Drops of crimson appeared but he paid no heed to anything but his storming passion for her.

They took a desperate second together to remove his trousers and spring his full length free of restraint. She attempted to grasp his thick and stone hard cock but he brushed her hand away. Then he took one of his large hands and with two sweeping motions, pinioned her wrists and then swung her arms over her head. She was his captive except for her legs. And her entire body quivered in the anticipation of his domination.

He bent to her neck and growled ferociously as he drew his fangs over it and down to her shoulders. It was a calculated move and he was particular to not seriously draw her blood. Yet he did draw enough and lapped at it with the pleasure of the passion-enslaved. His cock drooled clear dew onto her nether lips and that added to their combustion and need.

He did speak now as words had a uniqueness that inspired what thought would not. "Close your eyes and don't open them until I say!"

Her tremulous whisper ended in a gasp. "Yes, oh god yes, my love."

His cockhead flared as big as any mushroom cap that either had seen and the color of it and the prominence behind it was a beating dark red. The near cobalt of the vein that throbbed and whooshed added immensely to the sexual beat. And each throb lashed him with a greater craving for her and her flesh.

She took her legs and curled them past his hips to his buttocks. And she used them as a guiding force that thrust him forward and sank him deeply into her. She shivered uncontrollably as he plumbed her depths and rocked into and out of her rapidly. With each stroke in, his pelvis smacked hers and the vibration of that spread especially to her ruby red jewel.

She was flushed from her throat down to her upper chest. That flush made the bobbling movement of her breasts even more pronounced. Mikilenia found his target, one of her nipples, and sucked hard on it all while pumping her strong and holding her wrists in a lock which was unbreakable.

The heat between them escalated so rapidly now.

Her whimpers transformed into groans and she drew her lips back in sheerest ecstasy. Those lips trembled in the motion. Her exposed fangs aroused him and he hissed in pleasure and purposely revealed his polished fangs fully to her.

"Open your eyes now. Do it now!"

She was so spiked by her own sexual demand that she did not hear him and he had to repeat himself. With the second command, her eyes flew open.

It was when she viewed his monster fangs, felt his monster cock inside of her that a wave pounded through her body. That feeling was primal. It exploded outward and then contracted and she experienced a vortex of heavy bliss at her loins. It was so powerful that everything for her revolved around her cunt and its grip upon his pole.

She cried incoherently.

It was then that he shuddered and spilled himself into her. Their spasms matched and lifted them up intensely. He threw his head back and howled. She wept and was overcome. She shook and shook in the wonderful assault just transpiring.

Then, as he slowly removed himself, she dipped her fingers into her opening and then tasted their blend.

They held each other for a while.

Once past the spell of their lovemaking, they sought the sky.

Neither suffered the need to look back.

CHAPTER 39

A New Resident

The clouds scudded through this night's mordant horizons as a storm was setting to bristle over their heads. It was no cyclone though and it did not slow the motion of the bodies underneath the royal hut's roof. They lay casually atop the thick mats woven with the soft fronds of the ponga. This silver fern frond lay smooth for them and their wool blankets provided whatever warmth might be needed by them.

Tongea casually toyed with the serpent talisman that dangled from Anteekwa's left nipple. The contrast between the metal and the flesh was vivid. The pitch black quality of her enlarging nipple almost caused the small piece of jewelry to glow in its brownish red blend. And it had caught his attention many a time but this time, though passion-flicked, he asked about its origin.

She, on the other hand, was already finding his play, his twisting and turning of the amulet, to be so very distracting. She would answer him but yearned for his throb inside of her. Her flooded cleft, ripened red jewel and begging nipples would simply have to wait. This was her first opportunity to tell him of her tale at his request.

"Sweetness, if you are going to ask me these questions, you have to stop pulling on my serpent. Please. Otherwise it is difficult to concentrate. And it is already. So stop it now."

She threw her head back after commanding him and thrust her chest at him. He laughed and gave the tiny metal object a last tug. She quivered and then laughed in such a husky manner.

"I want to know. I want to know now, love. Start with the serpent and tell all to me." Tongea was trying to make this difficult for her as he still cupped the bottom of her breast and thumb stroked around her nipple so lightly.

She placed her hand on his and removed his from her altogether.

"This is a trinket of much significance to me, Tongea. I have worn it for at least two hundred years without ever considering its removal. Many fingers have dabbled with it but Mikilenia was who made me wear it. He swore me to a pact, if I never removed it, he would always be faithful to me. And, as you can attest, the ornament remains yet he does not; so much for promises from those who have false hearts.

"I come from an Indian people who may still reside along the intersection of three great rivers. I was a princess there and revered the city's chieftain . . . until the day that I met a stranger within our midst. And to answer your probable next question, yes it was Mikilenia.

"He enchanted me with his powers. He beguiled me with his promises. But I finally had to wear this for him before he would give me the same powers that he possessed. I wore it gladly and he made me immortal. And then I made you immortal. Or rather he also made you immortal as I was unaware of how quite to accomplish that for you. Now I know. And I will show you if you ever need to transform one who you deem deserving of infinite life."

"But the serpent Anteekwa, why a serpent?"

As he had teased her, she was returning the favor by telling him the origins of the trinket slowly.

"It was delicately hammered into being by a coppersmith in the copper mines that lay in our city. The city, Cahokia, was ample. It held many, many people like me. I don't know if that city still thrives but it did when I was forced to depart it. I went with Mikilenia and we did not look back then. Nor have I ever gone back there. My name, Anteekwa, means Black Raven in my culture's language. And, as the raven, I have wandered far. With his companionship, I have surmounted prairies and mountains and even found a wild sea like this one in the intervening years between then and now.

"Let me explain why he and I were forced to leave my beautiful city of the mounds.

"My people worshipped many gods. But the Snake Spirit of Life, the serpent that you view with fangs bared, whose prong bores through my nipple, was our god of fertility. And our clan, the tribe of Cahokia, found a time before each planting of the corn to sacrifice maidens to please this god. The goddess of corn was equally cherished and between the two, much blood was spilled. That ensured fertility of the crops and fertility of our Indian population.

"These maidens were young and virginal. They lived in a shelter upon one of the mounds, the most magnificent one, and were secured there so that their virginity was absolute and never open to chance defilement.

"With the influence of an insistent new love and what seemed a fundamental change in his soul, our leader demanded the elimination of the sacrifices and of the gods in one broad stroke. His proclamation affirmed that there was only one God. My paramour then, in a desire to wrestle rule from this Kakeobuk, incited rebellion and riot from within and without the city's boundaries. I am ashamed to say this to you in this moment Tongea, but I acquiesced and then participated in acts of destruction. And it was done to restore false traditions and bring Mikilenia to the city's supreme position. And neither of us cared who died or suffered in the process.

"It was all wicked, detestable.

"But the entity inside of Kakeobuk overrode us and cast our rebellion aside. His patience was gone and he ordered the two of us to leave. We were considered pariah ever after.

"Peering back into that time, I realize that I was just Mikilenia's pawn. And a very capable pawn I was. Woe that I did treachery against my own."

He queried, "And that was what your heart was fleeing from when my spear split the air around you and nearly brought you down."

"The spear would not have harmed me unless it was made of the Hawthorn tree. Anything other, unless the point was deadly silver, would have been simply removed by me with total healing to follow.

"You simply annoyed me and I was hungry even in my grief. Mikilenia had betrayed me as he had betrayed all those two hundred years ago.

"In retrospect, I excuse him as he was in the pangs of his own lost love. And it obviously drove him crazy. And I was so enamored that I was equally as crazy. But my unraveling, the final tearing of his and my alliance, cleared my sight. And the lucky discovery of you has restored my trust in my heart's judgment."

Tongea had an immediate gentle response, "And my life has been remade by you profoundly. I now have these." He displayed his fangs then. "And I have you. I do not ever want to part.

"Do you miss your home?" he asked her.

Anteekwa was pleased that he concerned himself with her deepest feelings. His culture sometimes backhanded women's involvement in anything except to obey the male's sexual commands. And once those needs were satisfied, they then relegated their women to doing what the men considered lesser valued domestic duties of child rearing and of managing the home's hearth. Unique was Tongea in this regard. His tendency was to desire equality between him and her.

And if he hadn't, she would have bitten him a severe one on his neck.

Her burning wish was to be with him as a new resident of the land that was his. It would become hers too and she was beyond excitement to realize that.

"Do you miss your home or will you stay with me here?" Tongea asked that with a sly smile on his face. He had asked just earlier and wanted an immediate answer. But he also felt wanton and playful with her. So, simultaneous with his somber toned question, he reached lovingly for her talisman and pulled it taut. Her nipple stretched and lengthened quickly. Her dark tip was already so thick but this caused even more engorgement and lengthening.

She moaned and kissed him hard. She panted and hardly found the way to say, "Of course, I will stay with you. Ahhhhhhh yes, you do that so well.

"Forever." She managed to moan that into his ear as her legs writhed and she reached for his stone heavy and much extended manhood.

He knew that she meant the forever.

CHAPTER 40

Dead Embers

The dead embers of burnt twig and log lay used and useless inside the circle of the once gigantic fire. This was what he felt like. His heart was now dead with useless ember where it had once been fierce flame that fed upon itself as if there was no end. But there was. And he had reached it.

In his sorrow, he almost wanted to believe that it was better to have never loved and be pain spared.

Then he thought back to the ravages of his life when love had been absent and he had no comprehension of any but wild and savage emotions. He was barbaric and the ultimate fearless warrior. He had been Mezopx of the rivers, Tigris and Euphrates. He was an Akkadian king and ruled ruthlessly until his capitol city of Akkad bent to the sword of the city of Ur.

By Akkad's demise, he had morphed and Mezopx had vanished. He had not understood initially but had transformed into something less than corporeal but something much more than just powerful. He had become an undead thing, an entity, which was almighty; except for the Almighty. He himself was ruled by that Invisible Hand. He chafed at being restrained in any fashion but he found that he had no choice in that realm. His master was absolute and he no longer resisted that long ago turn of events.

Mezopx had blinked out but the entity, at his master's behest, awaited a future that he was unable to envision. Finally, as Rome dominated the human horizon, he was released to occupy a petty spirited but very fortunate bureaucrat turned emperor named Septimius Severus. The entity had brought him luck in abundance.

And in all that span of time, he had not once felt an emotion that kindled positive sentiments. He was skilled at displaying anger, vengeance, a deep lack of compassion and an incomprehension regarding mercy. He was considered the dark lord in his time then as he was not witnessed ever in the light of day. And what was more natural than that for the icon of the undead!

How his blighted soul, yes the undead had them, survived with the smallest seed of empathy intact was beyond his reckoning here and now. But that seed had not only survived but suffused through him and allowed him to know that surreal emotion called love.

It had only been upon his third incarnation, brief though it was, as Eumann in Scotland's infancy that he had found a compelling desire for Catrione. But that sensation still was not as full as it would be when he was compelled to save the life of Cinead Mac Alpin by becoming Cinead Mac Alpin. That is when he realized what love was as he found his darling. Names meant nothing really but her name was Aiobheean then. And she was mortal. But she was not for long. And as she followed the entity, loving him as profoundly as he loved her, time and circumstances moved her to be called Minkitooni. And, obviously in this, their last adventure together, she was Janna.

He adored her but had lost her by his very imperfect honesty. He had coveted her so much that he had withheld some vital facts from her. That was what she discovered while they bled their love dry on the deck of the Heemskerck only several nights ago. But even to one who lived an eternity, that span since the collapse seemed an eternity.

So his heart was alone and lonely. Prior, his heart had been alone but lonely had been beyond his conception. Now his heart was his travail.

"Ah me, I am fucked." he sighed to himself.

Even if he went back to the ships, the four caskets that lay beneath his Master Commander quarters were only what he alone required. The three other boxes would lay barren. That notion lay heavily on him. But he had an obligation to his crew. They needed his guidance and he would see them back to safe harbor in Batavia.

The probability, without even using his sight, was that the crew was getting restless and anxious to ply the open sea again.

Enough of this island paradise he laughed. They all had languished long enough here and too much blood had been spilled. The entity would only miss the peaceable Te Moriori and their undeniably wise leader. Nunuku had held them spellbound with facts and legends of the islanders abounding. He embodied the profoundly wise and benevolent chieftain.

Oh, if only more were like him.

But Abel and his ships would fly from the shores of the entire multitude of islands jutting out of the crystalline waters surrounding. This was his newly found promise to himself.

So much of his thought in this moment was to lend him a distraction from and defense against his longing for his beauty, his paramour.

Why had he not stopped the wicked embrace of mother and son those many, many years ago?! Would that he had, and he could have, because he resided in the son then, this heap of woes upon them all would not be.

One mistake, like a stone to water, the ripples found themselves echoing over and over.

Why hadn't he stopped them? What made him soft then when he needed to be strong? Or, rather, still peaked by his attraction to Catrione. That must have been it! He had not gotten over his thrill with her. He capitulated to it just as her son had.

He moaned in his sadness. And then to be so devious as to let the truth between all of them lay fallow. Some would say that it really wasn't a lie. They would say that Aiobheean had not delved into the issue with him ever. But he could have told her. And the most ridiculous part of it all was that truly, he had no excuses. She had not been near or even vampire with seer sight when the mead had led the mother and son to copulate. So how would she have known even to ask unless she had been told of mother and son's disgraceful intersection?

No, he was guilty and deserved the consequences forthcoming. Like many a mortal and vampire alike, the illusion that one can dance away from the truth forever is such a seductive one. And yet, here the piper was; at his door.

It was time for him to put lock and clamp on his brain and cease the mental palaver, cease the whining. She was irrevocably gone and all that remained for him regarding her was to move along with memories intact.

So he shook himself from these blasted demented reveries.

He would have another pass at the islands, especially where the sweet, sweet lagoon was concerned, and then shake a leg and rouse his shipmates enough to disembark just before the sun rounded upon the landscape.

Shedding the human shape, he flew ceaselessly for many hours.

The lagoon did stir him and he had to rush from it before he was overcome.

With all speed, he worked the skies again and glimpsed the naked masts on the Heemskerck and the Zeehaen. With spirit lifted some at the sight of the vessels moored, the vessels that were his to command, he touched the planking and sought human form again.

Visscher and Gilsemans ran to where Abel had just appeared.

Almost in unison, they cried. "We thought that you might not return!" Their relief was absolutely clear to Abel.

And if Holleman, of the Zeehaen, had been on the Heemskerck too, he would have acted the same.

CHAPTER 41

Return Voyage

The sails had been hoisted and the anchors raised. Activity had exploded at Abel's command. And he commanded their departure as soon as he was capable of calming Visscher and Gilsemans.

"I cleave closely to my ships and crew. Of course, I returned.

"Give the orders to set forth into the open sea immediately. Enough of paralysis in this bay or this land. Away.

"Wake all. We are away!"

He had barked those words an hour ago and he stood at the bow of the Heemskerck and felt the salt spray whip his chin red. He understood this pain. It also served to distract him from the other deeper ache of his.

This return voyage would take a half year to complete and by the time that they reached the port of Batavia, they would be nearly overcome with exhaustion. And the causes of the continuously stretching fatigue were many.

Only days into their exodus from the Te Maori and their kingdom, their ships came across a flat finger of terrain whose soil was skimmed with tropical foliage as far as the eye could see. It was not viewed by Abel as it was the bright

221

of noon but his seconds anchored and paused long enough to have sketched the geography before them. The crew though, having just reset their sights on distant Batavia, was in no mood to linger.

As they put back to sea, they saw that all was not level though. There was a strong pitch of cliff that only gradually tapered to the sparkling turquoise waters. Once though that these sheer embankments disappeared into the luminous horizon, even small hillocks were not found within the green territory.

The wind was brisk and the air was sharp and cold. Yet, just before fully leaving this place, they managed to identify an enclosed lagoon or two. Birds massed and swooped in this area. Some flew low enough to nearly smack into the men holding the lookout positions. The squawking was intense and a single large albatross collided with the material of a smaller, higher sail.

The tear from that was heard and then its location determined. It took much of the early afternoon to lower their sails in that section, repair the slightly torn section and then to again raise it back. The delay bothered the superstitious and angered the impatient.

They wove through a multitude of tiny isolated islands and treacherous coral reef before freeing themselves from those particular dangers.

Abel learned of these sightings and their associated happenings by rifling through the navigators' journal at night's rising. He was pleased at the efficiency of the crew in fixing the sail and of having avoided foundering on the coral shoals.

No more had he thought that than those spectral silhouettes of a string of volcanic islands registered. And his special ability to view what others could not made him realize that there was still ample sharp coral just beneath the surface of the waves slapping at the Heemskerck and the Zeehaen. They were easily avoided when he was roused and active. He simply had to trust in Visscher, Gilseman and Hollemans' skills when he was bound into undead sleep.

Ironically therefore, day was more hazardous than the night.

Ah well, it couldn't be helped.

Open ocean proceeded next in their journey. Odd that a vast expanse of endless water meeting the cloud decorated heavens provided these men the comfort that they never seemed to find when foot touched the hard soil of civilization. Somehow, these sailors, these special men, understood their true origins. They intuited that they had come from the watery depths of these vast liquid regions; all humans had. But these particular individuals had a fierce desire to return to it. And even though Abel had different origins, he was proud to be among them.

Maybe it was the warm marine air that lulled them into a torpor and lassitude that would prove precarious for them. And, of course, Abel was below the Commander's Quarters, blind to all that occurred.

The wind kept them on a pace that also reassured the crew. And it was then that disaster reared up and screamed horribly in their faces. The Zeehaen, following behind the Heemskerck, avoided damage. Not so the Heemskerck.

The lookouts were aware of the broad and mountainous landmasses passing from bow to stern without incident.

It was at least three months since they had begun their return.

And they did forget the high rising coral that was still hidden by the sea surface.

The scrape against wood was loud and harsh. Immediately the shout to man all positions was heard round about the deck and lower quarters of the Heemskerck. Many below decks had heard the sound themselves and had instantly leaped to get above deck.

The Zeehaen, because it had been lumbering behind, recognized the distress of the forward ship immediately. Sails were rapidly repositioned and caught a breeze that allowed them to veer out of the same path that the Heemskerck had been following.

The men of the Zeehaen swarmed to their small boats and oared swiftly to where their sister ship was locked in position and was incapable of moving; sails and wind were of no use in this situation.

Stout ribs of wood, emergency items for an occasion where either ship might run aground were tossed from the Heemskerck to the oarsmen in the boats now dotted in the waves below. As the tide slapped against the stranded vessel, these poles were used to apply pressure upon the hull. The boats were unstable but not so much that, when a larger than usual wave popped against the ship's side, the creak of wood against wood added enough leverage to loosen the ship from the coral's grasp. The probability too was that much of the coral also crunched under the huge load that the Heemskerck applied to it.

Whatever fortuitous circumstance brought sudden good fortune, no one questioned their luck.

There were men who did remain below decks and they were scooping water that leaked through the hull and then others who, after having thrown those wood fulcrums to the men of the small boats, had gone back to their emergency stash and brought wood plugs and large hammers to the several thumb size holes and pounded those plugs securely into the open space. They wiped the area dry as possible and then painted a tar over the area. The seal was successful.

The excess wood plugs and the tar were returned to the stash. Many of the poles were lost in the mammoth effort. A few survived and were returned. The hope was that there was to be no further necessity for their use.

When Abel lifted the lid of his casket, the two ships were safely on their way.

They made land once more before being received in suitable fashion by the residents of Batavia. It was another island but was grander than all of the others combined. The ridge of snowcapped mountains seemed taller than any earlier observed. There was a distinct tree line on these stone monoliths with huge chunks of glaciers hugging above and at their hems.

The tropical rain fell hard and splashed onto the deck with unmistakable sound. The humidity was thick. It was difficult to believe that they were being bathed in warm water while looking at the chill of the white peaked mountains. The chill triumphed and they all shivered.

They witnessed nothing that resembled solid earth from that point forward.

The final leg for the ships ended on June fifteen of sixteen forty three.

And their exhaustion was well earned. They had discovered and experienced much.

They had enough energy to celebrate their welcome home.

Then they would sleep the sleep of the dead.

CHAPTER 42

Batavia Cheers

From the point of view of the Dutch East India Company, Abel's explorations were a disappointment so far. He had neither found a promising area for trade nor a useful new shipping route. The company was modestly upset that he didn't fully explore the lands that he found. They debated on whether to send another commander to navigate those waters again or whether they should send Tasman for a second attempt. They decided on the latter.

In the meantime, Abel and his crew ignored everything except that Batavia itself cheered their arrival and celebrated it with pride and gusto. For the shortest of time, they felt like heroes. And they reveled in it. It was considered improper to socialize with the lesser class of sailors and seamen but Abel, the entity actually, disregarded the prigs who ran the Dutch colony. Let them wear their lace and a powdered wig, the entity was going to have some fun. And he was bold in ensuring that Abel danced to the tune that was set by his undead inhabitant.

And it was during one of these joyous evenings, as Abel was in his cups that he sat with his body and head listing southward. It was then that he felt a painful ping inside of his head. Too much ale he thought and ignored the discomfort. The ping changed into a buzz and that sound was insistent and struck an ache internally just back behind his eyes.

The entity awoke suddenly to the fact that his master was signaling the end of this habitation. Abel was about to be abandoned. The entity was reluctant, as always, but had no choice in the plans laid out for him. And the buzz escalated into an urgent cacophony of sound, so shrill and discordant that the demands of the master must immediately be served by him.

Abel's body trembled and then seized spasmodically. His eyes closed and there arose a brief whooshing sound. Abel fell from his sitting position hard to the floor.

The entity was separate from the Tasman form that was prostrate and helpless. He moved so swiftly that the air hardly parted before him. His truest shape was what he was in this moment of transition. He was a tiny black mass containing a central circular repository of undead energy; writhing tendrils projected haphazardly from the hub of his form. He was not a spider he knew. Thank God. He hated this incarnation of himself almost as intensely as he hated his bat configuration.

Life was a bitch, even undead life. He knew not where his ultimate destination might be this time or how long the wait between this last skin and his next skin was to last.

Abel roused so slowly and was utterly confused as to why he was being assisted from the floor and, after feeling for his forehead, why he had blood on his fingers. He rubbed the slick, slippery substance between his fingers in an almost comatose disbelief.

Some of his sailing compatriots yanked him back up with less regard than they would have hoisted a sail.

"Ye just dropped down and cracked yer head, Master Commander. The brew here is a right too strong fer ya.

"Let's have at getting ya upstairs n safe within the bed."

This seemed like an utterly good idea to Abel. He simply wanted to rest. His weary body had finally had enough.

Once laid upon a soft flat surface, Abel passed out for many hours.

It was when he arose that he discovered his dry mouth and a headache that plagued him thoroughly. The knot on his head was hard and enflamed.

Still, he wanted to reclaim his dignity and dressed himself with the few items that the others had removed before they released him to the sheet, blanket and mattress.

His hands and fingers shook and those miniscule tremors slowed him more so as he tried to hurry.

He wanted to go immediately to his superiors and let them become aware that he was completely ready to perform valiantly in whatever they had devised for his future.

He stepped out into the bright sunlight.

He was assigned to return to the area that he had just left. So, in sixteen hundred forty four, he and a three ship crew took part in an expedition to form a Dutch settlement in what were later known as the Tonga Islands. And the plan was to afterward launch raids from those islands into Chile. And in addition to this, Tasman was tasked to find whether there was a passage into what was even then known as the South Sea between what is the current Australia and New Guinea.

The voyage of the three ships never did find that passage; a passage which would have made travel to South America that much easier.

After arriving once again at Batavia, his information brought him the reward of confirmation in his grade with a substantial increase in pay. This increase in pay reached all the way back to his venture in what became New Zealand.

He remained in Batavia and was soon enough appointed to Batavia's Council of Justice. But he was not able to sit still nor was the Dutch East India Company capable of leaving him alone.

In mid sixteen forty seven, he put out several ships on a mission to Siam. And this was quite the accolade as he was chosen over all other Dutchmen. It was a huge honor and he clutched it with all the strength available to him. He and the King of Siam made all sorts of covenants that were useful for trade and for the two countries long after.

Fortune was much less beneficent to Tasman in the years following.

He was given charge of eight lethal vessels that rode the waves in order to take down Spaniard sails. This Dutch tour de force was lackluster and it came to a draw eventually.

That was not what caused a temporary decline in The Dutch Commander's luck. An incident on board during the warring ships encounters seemed a trivial sort of thing. If not trivial, it was not an expansive act that put his larger culture at risk. Proceedings were taken against him once arrived in Batavia for having treated one of his sailors in a barbarous way.

He was drunk when the incident occurred. And for this, at the governor-general's pleasure, he was removed from office altogether.

Upon appeal some years later, he was given his commander's status back and the blot, the taint, on his record was pushed aside by a more lenient governor-general. In his later years, Tasman was a religious, loyal and hardworking individual. His exemplary behavior persuaded the latter Batavian regent to forgive Tasman's single professional error.

His reinstatement occurred in sixteen fifty one but he became ready to lay his office, his sword and his limbs down. He gave up work, therefore, in sixteen fifty two. He had difficulty finding a sense of quiet calmness so he abandoned the lassitude of retirement and promptly went into business as a Batavian merchant.

As with almost everything else, the business endeavor was wildly prosperous and he came into an affluence that secured the welfare of him and his descendants at length.

It was in sixteen fifty nine that he performed his duties one evening, sank into his bed and then never lifted his head again.

The entity observed this from his underground perch nearly two hundred years after his involuntary leave-taking from Abel and the southern hemisphere.

CHAPTER 43

Grave Sadness

That a black blob sheltering in the recesses of a cave's guts could not only be one of the most powerful forces in the world but also a being of growing sensitivity, even the light of empathy shone brightly for him on more and more occasions, was beyond most anyone's imagination. He comprehended that. Nonetheless, known or not, imagined or not, he was very real and pulsated with energy in the dank subterranean folds of a rocky European earthen fissure.

He had been holed up on a ledge that had been created by the steady fall, drop by drop, of water on the limestone within. He was perched and ready to burst from this place when his master gave him that opportunity. He had been forced to shelter here for nigh on to two hundred years. He saw the year that it was in the vibrations that were his seer sight. It was almost the midpoint of the nineteenth century.

He protected himself from the sheer and utter monotony of his situation by taking one of two avenues. The first was an action of fierce and compelling necessity. That was his body's demand for the renewal of blood within his system nightly. And, though he was diminutive and not corporeal, he still required the same amount of blood to sustain himself as he needed when inside of a skin. So he left the cave as often as his belly urged him to. The second was an action of his ever spinning mind. And the fact that he was an endlessly curious creature as well. This was his desire when strongly girded emotionally; and two hundred years had finally brought him to an acceptable emotional strength to envision Nunuku, Ahuriri and their land's evolution. So he finally chose to look back at the events that had shaped him as he explored the shores of the kingdom that they had discovered while journeying down under.

A potential for grave sadness lurked there in this profoundly necessary project of his. He had to grasp what had happened to those he had met; those whom he considered wise and special friends. And the larger cultures too, what of them also?

Nunuku loomed so large as an image inside his skull that the entity had to deal with the Te Moriori first and foremost. And it was as he suspected. As usual, peaceful practices gave way to the violent and merciless. This was even worse than he had feared. He cringed but sought out the inevitable outcome. It was a slaughter and the Te Maori had overcome.

Was this the destiny of human civilization he thought? The irony of his being other than human and concerning himself with a passion for the welfare of that species did not escape him. But his heart had thawed radically in his encounters with each of mankind's various peoples.

He was loath to let the details of the near extinction of the tribe that dwelled upon what he grasped was called Chatham Island. Yet his mind was too weak to close the door of images once it had been opened a crack. The door was flung back and the images rocketed into his brain. He flattened himself against the ledge and all movement of his tentacles stopped in the onslaught. It was as if he were under the heel of a massive boot.

After the Te Maori had blistered the waves and outpaced the cyclone, they beached themselves on the rough and rocky shores of the Te Moriori. The islanders there watched their few points of easy entry for exactly that reason. And here it came.

One of the Te Moriori lookouts sped back to Nunuku's village to report the ill news. And Nunuku, though his decision was set, chose to hear his members out. He never desired to have an absolutely closed mind. And he presented the situation to them. "The Te Maori are at our borders. And they are savages who have no respect for a peaceable style. They will kill us without hesitating, they will enslave the survivors or, if any of those survivors are disabled or weak, they may eat them.

"The question is, should we resist or maintain our allegiance to the principle of life without violence?"

There was no hesitation, the entity could see. All Nunuku's advisors supported the concept of a civil attitude of cooperation and compromise at all costs. And so none of his people were allowed resort to brute force or killing.

And here is how it went. The entity was ripped by deep emotion.

Te Moriori men were slaughtered like sheep, a large portion of those peaceable and dignified people were ritually put to death, a ritual that included staking out women and children on the beach and leaving them to die in severe pain over several days. Nunuku, as chieftain, was staked but staked separately from his followers. As chieftain, the Te Maori, in their twisted thinking, believed that his prominence required the dignity of death out of sight.

Possession of the land was taken and new laws were pronounced. The Te Maori invaders forbade the speaking of the Te Moriori language. They forced those males who were still alive to urinate and defecate on the sites that the Te Moriori held sacred. And Te Moriori were refused the right to marry or have children with any Te Maori individual; not that this was a hardship for the conquered. Slavery was tightly enforced and rigidly maintained.

And as time passed, the Te Moriori was assimilated into the Te Maori society. And their near total annihilation was ensured.

The entity shook and nearly dissolved into himself. Empathy just about murdered his already hard existence in this cave. But, huge irony that it was, he would rather have suffered this tenderness anytime than to ever be Mezopx again.

He had to cease his scrutiny of the past for a while to recapture some kind of calm.

And then began again.

There was an explorer like Tasman who touched on New Zealand boundaries. He was more willing to involve himself and his crew in the process of familiarizing them with the Te Maori culture than Abel had been. Tasman, with the entity's strong persuasion, had vastly favored the Te Moriori and their ways. Ironic! The entity was bewildered often by the twists and turns of the quality that humans called empathy. But he was finding that regardless of his ambivalence in that emotional whirlpool, he preferred letting it seep into him.

Mystery, mystery; there was just too much mystery!

Two more times this brave adventurer returned to the region. He did no harm and gave to the Te Maori much beyond what he took.

Then a portion of the North Island and a sizeable chunk of the North Island's Te Maori population were destroyed by a disease of some kind. He wondered if this had been brought by the influx of Europeans to what was a truly beautiful territory. He eventually surmised that it was not brought by them because the Europeans had settled amongst the natives long ago. How then?

Yet the Europeans consisted, up to this moment, of nothing other than males. No woman had dared venture to such a wild place. And the men had desired such. If there were to be intermarriage, the sly European male desired that they commingle with the Te Maori women only. To risk the reverse was to risk ruination.

But then she finally reached this seemingly forbidden terrain. And life changed radically.

The coming of the female had nothing to do though with the next evolution of circumstance. Muskets were brought exclusively by male Europeans and given to the Te Maori without any pretense at encouraging wise and judicious use of the weapon. So many natives died musket blast after musket blast.

Blood was everywhere. The undead drew blood to themselves out of necessity and an irresistible urge. Humans drew the same to themselves for reasons that were voluntary and brutal. This was his opinion and he had felt it wherever he went. And he wondered how these humans had survived in the world for so long.

He parlayed next with the images of sheep, cattle, horses and poultry being introduced. These creatures thrived on the land and, yes, they multiplied in abundance.

Finally, he found a last view that did justice to the Europeans, at least. A first white child was born. Its squall was no different than any other child's. That pleased him for some reason.

His look back was over. Now just the wait settled upon him.

Oh for his master's call.

CHAPTER 44

Dream's Call

He had no eyes as the vibrating mass that he was. But, with his abilities, he saw further and better than any being, animal or human, could.

And every day, he closed those nonexistent eyes and fell into a slumber that was the equivalent of anesthesia. But, if the dream were strong enough, they breeched that shield.

This one was strong enough.

And the dream's call astounded him.

The light arose as if it was being blasted from a trumpet's shape, narrow initially and then expanding explosively into an ever widening circle of perfectly clear brilliance. The margins were stark and invisible in an unending darkness. His recumbent mind grasped what he might not otherwise had the dream's power been less.

The unconscious reverie brought him up short to a city that dazzled with its spires, domes and massive sprawling buildings. The shock of ornate and improbably large churches, veined in gold filigree, was instant. The dream veered from the spiritual monstrosities as the undead spirit within hissed and spit. Human divinity, though not fatal, was anathema to any vampire.

The rain poured down in sheets throughout the magnificent avenues that wove through the unknown metropolis.

Touching the outskirts were distinctly different bodies of water. One was a rolling river that wound in a path beautiful and blue. The other was a gulf that gouged out the land mass into a semicircle; an isthmus was its result.

The rain was replaced by a foggy swirl that drew his mind in.

It took but moments to penetrate this loose maelstrom of white. And when the dream did, the view was filled with what seemed to be that of a young male, pale in complexion, dark hair surrounding and a stance of strength and yet a delicate balance. The clarity was unusually visible in detail; beyond what most dreams could muster. This dream went beyond any previously experienced over his long and reaching years.

It was as if the dream brought the dreamer to some central pivot point and then rotated the view from the vantage point of the circle's hub. And the view was more than sumptuous, it was grand and powerful. The auditorium itself was vast. Colors shone brilliantly in this dream and the auditorium's majority was of a royal azure blue. Then there was the opulent splendor that peppered the interior throughout.

The dream held steady and so much was highlighted in an instant. Velvet and gold decorations stretched up each aisle and hung on each wall. Chandeliers were beautifully wrought and dangled strategically. Portraits of unknown men, men in uniform, men who demanded a salute were prominent. And the double headed eagle insignia were interspersed everywhere.

And then there were stately boxes for significant individuals to display themselves in. The boxes had elaborate arches and sliding curtains to manipulate exactly as one required.

The dream shifted without warning then.

The dreamer had to assume that time had elapsed as the young man and a woman of vivid appearance laughed in hushed tones backstage. They were alone in this huge palace of opera and ballet. Their hush was reflexive and was unnecessary. But they were engaged in something wonderful.

But who was he? And who was she? The dream was not willing to tell.

He watched the dream woman become the heart of the dream. It was no longer his vision but hers; her perspective for sure. It happened though to be occurring inside of his head.

She took his dream back to an onstage performance that was replete with dancers, her and him at the head of them all. She felt her slim form twirl and spin, appendages balanced, then leaping. By the operetta's design, she came deliciously into his arms. Through the openings in her mask, she drank him in. His big body with his handsome face leading her caused her to yearn and need that freedom to touch his long, flying black hair. She restrained herself, even in the surreal chambers of his mind's inner core.

A crescendo splashed onto the stage; bodies in furious motion. She swooned as he held her waist and lifted her higher and higher. They floated upward and she was enamored of him. He was her dream. But she questioned his love for her.

A parade of obscure images flew past.

He remained a dream observer. She was holding sway.

She and this man were enlivened by one another's touch.

He sucked at one of her aroused and so sensitive nipples. He was her lover and she arched her chest up to his hands as he swept them over her dancer's garments. She was on the stage floor, wood tightly laid together, hip and chest trembling in his direction. Her head was flung back and, by this, she signaled his possession of her.

She had allowed him, begged him, to strip her. He had nearly done so when she writhed and had to offer herself up to him immediately. Her tights remained as she fondled his erection through his still fully clothed form.

She itched to find her way past his clothing as she continued to rub his instrument and as he desperately sought one nipple after another to squeeze, twist and suckle through the thin material. Her breasts were heaving, rising and falling as she gripped his long locks with an almost maniacal fervor. Then she cupped the back of his head and pressed him deeply down upon her highly mounded breasts. He kissed over them spasmodically and needed to hold them in his palms.

It remained her dream. And in this dream of hers he had big hands with thick fingers. Yet those same fingers were mostly agile and delicate. And their touch ignited her desires. He tore at her top and ripped them down below her waist. Then, while she wiggled and lifted her hips, he got them almost off. She kicked the final clinging cloth over her ankles and feet.

Somehow, in this impossible dream, he was suddenly magically nude exactly as she was. And further magic was that, the entire dream was backlit by a blazing fireplace fire. The heat and crackle were beginning to overtake the dream. But she was tenacious and the dream held.

His dream observer was amazed at her strength. Her beauty was vast; her strength was more.

She and he were still fused to one another. Those delicate probing fingers of his dipped into her molten center and then spread her shiny nether lips wide. Her pulse was raging.

This sensation devoured her. Or was it he who devoured her? The lines of recognition were acutely blurred. He aroused her pulse further as he ascended to her carotid. What was that; that quick lancing pain? Oh she was devastated. He gulped at her neck, draining her of god's liquid. She fell into his embrace fully and even as the sucking sounds went on and on; her pulse would not stop rising. The background fire became the foreground flame. And it licked at everything until nothing remained.

He was stunned as nightfall came to the world outside the cave.

Yet his dream felt more alive than anything he felt once awake.

CHAPTER 45

New Skin

It was his manner of gently exhorting her to perform at levels beyond what she believed that she could. He was well aware that she had felt deficiencies in her last performance and was angry with herself. She was a perfectionist after all; yet he wanted to quell her impossible demands on herself but, in tandem, also lift her above the quality of her last effort.

He spoke to her in fluent but simple terms. She was not a native Russian and he had to be very careful that, as he spoke to her in the language that he wanted her to learn, she comprehended his meaning thoroughly. She was like a sponge in her stretch with information that she regarded highly. And she regarded his words and his teaching skills as consummate.

"We are doing Giselle, yes?"

She spoke in somewhat halting Russian, "Yes, of course we are Marius."

"Then you must feel Giselle's every sensation so that you can act out her every nuance.

"For example, when she returns from the grave, she is a ghost. Let yourself feel what it might be like to be a ghost who loves the human male before her. Your moves as you dance and pirouette, as you are en pointe, must reflect the looseness of a ghost, the infirmity of a ghost, the fragility of a ghost. Move daintily but a tiny bit like a rag doll. Be in total control of your body but make it appear otherwise. Be slightly disjointed.

"This will also give the audience the idea that you waver, almost visible but nearly on the verge of disappearing.

"And it will add wistfulness to your carriage, as if you are uncertain of your physical and emotional state.

"Finally, bend slightly at your waist, step backwards and then forwards barely. Hold your arms closer to your body than you would usually do. This will give the image of you shrinking.

"Ghostly, my love, that is all that Giselle's spectral being needs to convey."

She nodded slowly, thoughtfully.

Then, as it was a rehearsal where they were practicing alone, she tiptoed loosely to the stage of the Imperial Theater.

And it was while he watched her renewed efforts at capturing Giselle in a climactic moment that the Maestro felt a ping of quick and darting sensation part the molecules of his ribs. And then for only an instant longer his body yielded to a swift spread of vibration throughout him.

He grabbed at his side momentarily and gasped just once. In seconds, the clarity of his vision was acute and penetrating now where it had not been before. He had to adjust and the entity would make sure that he did.

The entity had roused from his dream. It had been a foreshadowing. His master had been kind rather than cruel to him and had come to him shortly after the dream. The skinless demon was not forced to wait long after the delicious morsel of that dream had massaged his spirit. The dream was brought to reality so rapidly.

Only days after the dream, with dark night settled upon his portion of the world, the hum of his master's command began. Though it was loathsome and loud to him, it also gave him the joy that he was to inhabit a new skin soon. The hum escalated and it became a shrieking scream that only he could hear. And he was profoundly aware that it would not cease until he found his target; his master's target actually.

It sent him exploding from his dank and dark hole into the heavens above. And the rush both actually and emotionally was huge. The shriek inside prompted him to use his finest interior radar and followed whatever lessened the reverberating sounds inside.

And it was through the roof of a masterfully built theater that he descended. The relief of diminished shriek motivated him sharply and he found the body that was now his. Tall, strong and dark, this habitation would do oh so well.

Marius inhaled acutely as he observed Viktoria dance her way beautifully into the spirit of Giselle. This was the very woman in the dream the entity knew. Could it be that she was even lovelier than she had been in the mists of his mind?

With the entity's power, he scrutinized her with eyes that were faster and more adept. And it caught him breathless. He had to release air from his lungs slowly in order to not look the dumbstruck fool.

She had materialized in his world of theater and choreography wildly. She had stepped into his domain and overwhelmed him without speaking a word of the language of St. Petersburg. His first thought had been that she was a gypsy and would be nothing more than a will o' the wisp.

And that had not been born out. She stayed and evolved into a performer of a magnificent natural ability. Her voice was rough to begin but sweetened incredibly with tutoring. And even that did not take long.

She conquered both his mind and his heart.

But it was her physical attributes that elevated all of his senses. His blood coursed wickedly when he carelessly let his guard fall. At that point, his erection was long and thick and there was no hiding it. Its fullness intruded upon his ability to move and dance freely. So he exerted harsh control over his desire for her as he could.

But he could not now. The entity was profoundly impacted and there was no stopping the appendage filling and the demanding throb that took hold.

He pulled a nearby chair to him with much haste. He did not want to embarrass himself, even in front of his lover. And so he sat and shifted enough to hide his reaction to her.

Her flow of shining black hair, subtle wave upon wave, riveted his attention. And then there was her face. He was branded by her face. And marveled at the smooth and flawless skin there, the angular majesty of her cheekbones and the magnetic fullness of her rose hued full lips.

Beneath, her ebony globes were tightly restrained for the sake of her performance. But he realized their qualities. Without the minimal corset that she wore presently, he understood what would be. And that was this. Her ebony globes would hang from her chest perfectly. They were full, finely copious, and pendulous. And prominent atop these mounds were dark aureoles that painted most of each mounds forward curve. Her nipples were long and thick even before stimulation occurred.

Her tight belly, firm ass and tapering legs, well-toned, served the completion of the erotic composition before him. And she was so sexual even when she was intending other.

She could have been the ugliest wench alive though and the entity would still have been pleased. He had tasted love and now did not want to live without it. And love was primarily an interior impulse. Beauty was a set aside. Cherished if it was there but it was not of necessity.

And he had an opportunity again.

He typically came to his fresh incarnation with an attitude of . . . it's about fucking time!

Not this round. He soundlessly thanked the Hand that had guided him.

That would be his attitude forevermore.

ABOUT THE AUTHORS

Jeffrey Underwood graduated from the University of Washington with a degree in psychology. Though he has practiced as a Registered Nurse for many years, he comes from a family of published authors. His first published work was The Forbidden Tome; Hansel and Gretel's True Tale. His second was entitled Lethal Assumed; Lost Tome Found. This is his fifth book and his third that encompasses true historical fiction. He currently resides in Mountlake Terrace, Washington, a suburb of Seattle and again hopes that those who read this fifth offering enjoy the time spent.

Kate Taylor collaborated with Jeffrey Underwood on two prior novels, entitled Treason's Truth; Mac Alpin's Scotland and Eagle's Eclipse; America Before Columbus. This present collaboration is her third with Jeffrey. This book is entitled Tasman's Travail; The Journey Down Under. Kate is nationally certified as an Activities Director. While she has worked in healthcare for many years and won awards for her service there, she is also talented in the world of watercolor and enjoys playing the piano. This work is her fourth serious effort at writing as her first work is entitled The Pink Eraser. She has contributed to books in the Activities profession. They say that no one lives in New Hampshire, but Kate does, and she has much in the way of writing to share. She hopes that all who read this tale of fiction and much fact will want for more.

On a playful level, Kate and Jeff have also combined in writing Rule of Thumb & Fingers, a texter's bible with lots of laughs and Sock Monkey Life which is full of sheer creativity.

Jeff and Kate met online and found that their collaborative interests meshed splendidly and this novel is an example of that blending of gusto for writing that they certainly both have.